OLEANDER

Jennifer Allis Provost

BELLATRIX PRESS

Bellatrix
Press

For the real life Feline Federation. Never stop biting ankles!

Contents

Chapter 1

Corpse Flowers

The office phone rang. Again.

"I can't believe you're still paying for that landline," my best friend and assistant, Tessa, yelled from the kitchen. "Cut that cord and save some money."

Ring. "And take work calls on my cell?" I yelled back. "Then they'd be able to reach me all day and night."

"They?"

Another ring. "You know. Them. Clients."

The current potential client in question was Bennet Carrington, who was the head horticulturist at the liberal arts college on the edge of town. He was an old friend of my grandmother's, and he'd been calling my office for the past two days about a situation at his greenhouse he thought I should investigate. Being that I already had a full caseload, Tessa deflected him at every turn, but he kept calling back and leaving ever-urgent messages. When Tessa turned off the answering machine, he countered by putting us on speed dial. I was being stalked by a middle-aged gardener.

After the seventh ring, Tessa shouted, "You might as well pick up. He's just going to hang up and call again."

I sighed and picked up the receiver. "Nine Lives Investigations."

"Eliza, you simply must come to the greenhouse! It's happening!"

"What is happening, Bennet?"

"The corpse flowers! They're about to bloom!"

I sighed again, or maybe it was just my brain leaking. "If they're flowers, shouldn't they be blooming?"

"You don't understand. Under normal circumstances amorphophallus titanum only blooms once every ten years or so, but all three of my specimens are set to bloom tonight."

"Tonight, huh? Exactly how do you know that?"

"I am a horticulturist," Bennet replied frostily. "If you must know, the specimen's spathe typically unfurls in early afternoon, and things move rather quickly after that. Full inflorescence should be achieved by midnight."

"Ooo-kay. So we have corpse flowers getting corpse-y. Exactly what do you want me to do about it?"

"Don't you think the sheer number of pending blooms, coupled with the day after tomorrow's most auspicious date, warrants a deeper investigation?"

I glanced at the calendar. "The day after tomorrow is Sunday. Will the flowers be going to church?"

"Sunday is April Fools' Day! As you know, certain non-corporeal beings do delight in playing tricks on such, what do you call them? Ah, yes. Fake holidays."

I pinched the bridge of my nose and wondered if it was too late to change careers and become an accountant. Math had always been one of my best subjects, and I was pretty good with spreadsheets. "I still don't understand what you expect me to do about this. I'm a private investigator, and I really don't see anything that needs investigating."

"Yes, but you take on special cases," he said, emphasis his. "And we're all well aware of how you assisted in the belladonna caper a few months ago, and that you received assistance from a ghost."

I laughed, partly because he'd used the word caper, but mostly because busting out with nervous laughter was my defense mechanism whenever anyone brought up my talent for interacting with the dead. So far, it hadn't fooled anyone.

"How did you hear about that?" I asked.

"Believe it or not, I do spend time outside of this greenhouse."

"All right, I'll come down."

"Wonderful. The greenhouse closes in half an hour. With the patrons gone we'll be able to speak privately."

"See you then."

I replaced the receiver on the cradle, then I let my head drop into my hands. Of course, Bennet knew about the belladonna incident. All the local gardeners must get together for Sunday brunch and gossip about current events over hot cups of chamomile tea. He was also one of the people who knew I was a seer, meaning that I could see ghosts and exorcise demons. It wasn't shocking that he knew about my supernatural talents seeing as how he'd been close to Gran, but I'd been trying to stay as low-key as possible. Now, thanks to some stupid corpse flowers it seemed like he would be getting an in-person confirmation of those rumors.

Wonderful.

***

It took me about an hour to get to the college, and it was another fifteen-minute walk across the campus to get to the horticultural department's new greenhouse. The college itself was a typical mid-century modern edifice, complete with a rectangular central green and a row of boxy dorms off to one side. All in all, it was a rather forgettable institution of higher learning.

The greenhouses, however, were the real deal. Whoever had designed them had gone for authentic-looking Victorian splendor, and had probably bumped up the average student's tuition bill by a few grand in the process. The central greenhouse was an elongated oval, and two rectangular portions were attached to the center points of the oval. The bottom third of the exterior walls was made of stacked gray stone, while the rest of the walls and the roof were shining panes of glass held together with iron frames. There was even some wrought iron scrollwork standing along the center roofline, and all of the metal trim was painted a gleaming white.

I wondered who was in charge of washing all those windows.

I found the door, which was a stately oak slab fitted with an antiqued brass handle and matching hinges, unlocked. As the door creaked open I was hit with a wall of warm, humid air that smelled like a bouquet on steroids.

I poked my head inside the dimly lit interior. "Hello?" I called. "Bennet?"

"Yes?"

The owner of the voice appeared so suddenly he startled me. He was a thirtyish man with broad shoulders, serious gray eyes behind wire-rimmed spectacles, and blond hair held down with a year's worth of pomade. He was dressed in a tweed suit complete with a waistcoat and tie, and I wondered how he wasn't sweating to death in the greenhouse's warmth.

"Hi, I'm looking for Bennet Carrington," I said. "I have an appointment with him."

"Ah. Of course," he said in his pseudo-British accent. My grandmother used to call that sort of inflection a Brahmin accent. Tessa referred to it as regular people trying to sound important. "This way, please." He pivoted on his heel and beckoned me to follow him down the narrow aisle. "Forgive me my confusion, but when you called out I misheard you, and assumed you were looking for me."

"Is your name Bennet, too?" I asked.

"No, it's Nicholas. Nicholas Allwood, assistant horticulturist." He glanced at me and tipped an imaginary cap. "At your service, miss?"

"Moore. Eliza Moore," I replied, doing my best James Bond impression. "My friends call me Eli."

"Very well, Miss Moore." He paused, then continued, "You should really address Dr. Carrington by his honorific. Quite a lot of work is involved in becoming a master horticulturist. Referring to him as Dr. Carrington affords him a well-earned measure of respect."

"Oh, I've always just called him Bennet," I said. "I've known him since I was a kid. He's an old family friend."

"Understood."

We reached a sliding glass door, and Nicholas paused with his hand on the latch. "Miss Moore, I feel the need to warn you that certain specimens in this room are quite pungent. Would you care for a handkerchief to cover your nose?"

If he only knew of the many times I'd had my olfactory nerves assaulted by various foul scents, demonic and otherwise. "Thanks, but I can handle it."

He nodded. "As you wish," he said, then he pushed open the door. The smell wafted toward me and I grimaced, and I remembered that corpse flowers were named as such because they smelled like rotting meat. While it was far from the worst odor I'd ever experienced, it was pretty rank in there.

"You'll find Dr. Carrington straight back, past the birds of paradise," Nicholas said.

"There are birds in the greenhouse? How do you keep them from eating all the plants?"

Nicholas's eyes narrowed. "Bird of paradise is the common name of the strelitzia family of plants."

I grinned. "I know. Just teasing you, Nick."

"I gathered that. Good day, Miss Moore."

Nicholas shut the door behind him, and I peered into the room. The interior of the greenhouse was stretched out before me, filled with bright flowers and glossy green leaves. The center aisle of the room was a cement path, and each side was packed with large potted plants and some honest to goodness trees set right in the dirt. Vines clambered up the trunks and lazily draped across the ceiling, completing the jungle effect. The place reminded me of my grandmother's solarium; if she'd had it her way her indoor garden would have been just as overgrown, if not more so.

I picked my way around the vines and tree trunks, and soon enough I found Bennet seated at a potting bench as he reviewed a few pages of handwritten notes. If Nicholas Allwood had presented as an uptight academic, then Bennet Carrington was on track to win Stuffed Shirt of the Year. He was also clad in a three piece tweed suit, though he had removed his jacket and carefully folded it before laying it on the stool beside him. He was wearing shiny wing tip shoes, round horn-rimmed spectacles, and as I approached him he was checking the time on an actual gold pocket watch that was secured to his vest with a matching chain.

"Hi Bennet," I said. "I'm here to hear all about your corpses. Corpse flowers, that is."

"Eli," Bennet shut the pocket watch's case with a clack and slipped it inside his waistcoat pocket. "Thank you so much for coming. I didn't hear you enter."

"Nicholas let me in," I said as I claimed the third stool. "Is having a posh accent a requirement to get into fancy gardener school?"

"Would that it were," he replied. "Now, Eli, I have been making some calculations, and I believe we're in for something very dire."

"Dire?" I repeated. "You still haven't fully explained why you called me about these weird plants in the first place. It can't be because of what happened with the belladonna at the retirement home."

"You're right. The belladonna had nothing to do with my reaching out to you." Bennet put down his pencil, then he removed his glasses and faced me. "When your grandmother was still alive, and it appeared that something otherworldly was soon to occur, I'd consult with her before moving forward. I was under the impression that such consultations now went to you."

I bit my lip, then I turned away. "Consult" was a polite way of saying he'd used to hit up Gran, the highest-ranking seer in the area, whenever something looked a wee bit magical. Gran had kept me shielded from what she did for most of my early years. I was thirteen before I realized that more ghosts than humans came to our house for Sunday dinner.

But realize it I did, and Gran explained that we belonged to a family of seers. In the old days we'd worked for kings, helping them pick auspicious dates for battles and locate prime sites for castles and temples. Nowadays most people thought that seers were either frauds or crazy, which is why I rarely talk about the family business to outsiders. But—and there's always a but—Bennet and Gran had been friends for years, and he attended plenty of Gran's events. However, I'd never once discussed anything supernatural with him. Hell, this was the first time I'd even spoken to Bennet since I'd returned to the area shortly before Gran's death, save for a few words we exchanged at her funeral.

"And why would you think that?" I asked. "I'm not Gran, I don't do what she did. I'm a private investigator."

"An investigator that specializes in extraordinary cases," Bennet said. "Or should I say, an investigator that delivers extraordinary results?"

Nervous laughter bubbled up my throat. I tamped it down, and said, "The cases I take aren't all that interesting. They're all cheating spouses and insurance fraud."

"I am referring to the rescue of Abigail Stevens."

I blew out a breath and looked up at the ceiling through the tangle of leaves. The reason I became a private investigator was because it is really hard to hold down a nine-to-five job when you could be visited by a clutch of demons, newly-dead ghosts or worse, ghost hunters, at any given time. At least the ghost hunters were manageable; I usually pointed them in the right direction and they went on their way. When a ghost latched on to me, now they were the worst. They never took no for an answer, and since they had nothing but time it was no big deal for them to hang around making my life miserable until I did whatever they wanted me to do.

Because of the constant intrusions into my life I needed to be my own boss, and becoming an investigator was the easiest, fastest way to make some money. It wasn't too hard to get the proper licenses and set up an office; it was even easier to find work, and soon enough I was making a good living. Then Abigail was kidnapped, and a ghost told me where to find her.

When little Abby Stevens was taken from her bed in the middle of the night it was all anyone talked about for days. Local law enforcement and her parents refused to give up searching for her, confident that she was still alive. As for me, after the first forty-eight hours had passed I'd assumed the worst. Then one of the ghosts who frequents the coffee shop in my building mentioned that Abby was being held in the back of an eighteen-wheeler, and the reason the cops couldn't get a lead on her was because her kidnappers kept the rig moving. The ghost, who'd had nine children of her own before she'd died of polio, then told me the truck's plate number, and where it usually refueled. Against all common sense, I went after the kidnappers alone, found the truck, and got Abby to safety.

The media went crazy, touting me as a savior to lost children everywhere. The story I'd told the reporters, and the police, had been simple out of necessity—I'd seen the plethora of news reports on Abby and was familiar with her appearance, then I happened to stumble upon the kidnappers at a truck stop, where they were letting Abby use the restroom—since telling the truth of how I'd found her wasn't really an option. The cops hadn't really believed that I'd found her based solely on random chance, but they were in no position to argue with me. After all, I'd found the kid and brought her back alive when they hadn't even known where to look.

Ever since the details of Abby's rescue had gone public my phone had been ringing off the hook. I got so many clients I could finally afford an assistant, and hired my friend Tessa to keep the books and set up appointments. I also moved to a larger apartment that had room for an office area up front. I stayed in the same building though, since the coffee shop that occupies the first floor was too perfect to part with.

Once I was set up in my new, more official office I carefully screened my cases, and didn't take on anything with a hint of the supernatural. People being what they are, I never had to wait long for an ordinary disgruntled person to hire me. I also avoided cases that might have me cross paths with the cops, since I knew that one cop in particular, Detective Daniel Lyons, was itching to finger me as a criminal; he'd never bought my story of how I'd found Abby, and he wasn't shy about sharing his opinions. Those factors meant that I took on a lot of boring cases, but whatever. It was a living, and the living was good.

Then there was the incident at the retirement home, which had been my first case. The residents were dropping like flies, and with the help of a few ghosts I found the killer. At the time no one thought I was anything other than a good detective, but after I found Abby I had to deal with a fresh batch of questions from the local police. I was rapidly running out of get out of jail free cards, and if I went along with Bennet and helped him figure out what sort of creature could be summoned by multiple corpse flowers blooming at once, I might play the last one.

But, what if something bad really was about to happen, and I could stop it?

"Okay. Fine. Let's say you're right, and I'm running the family business," I began. "I still can't do anything about these weird flowers. I know literally nothing about those plants."

"You don't need any horticultural knowledge for this situation," Bennet replied. "What I need is for you to assist me in containing whatever being they summon."

I glanced at Bennet's face; he was calm, as if he'd encountered such beings before. "You've done this before. Contained things."

"I have."

"Any idea what this being could be?" I asked. No sense in beating around the bush when this creature's—whatever it may be—arrival was imminent. I'd sort out Bennet's role in all of this after we'd dealt with it.

"It really could be anything," he replied. "Historically, groupings of three or more objects were used to summon demons, but I suppose any sort of spirit could manifest."

"Like a ghost?"

"Well, yes. That is a possibility."

Ghosts. I could handle a ghost. Other types of spirits, not so much. "May I see the flowers?"

"Of course."

Bennet led me to the center of the greenhouse where the corpse flowers were arranged in a circle, along with some palm trees and other specimens that looked straight out of a jungle. The corpse flowers were each planted in their own large, and rather ornate, cement pots, and the ground beneath the pots was covered with dark gray gravel. There was a small fountain in the center of the display, and the moon was shining directly onto the water's surface.

The corpse flowers themselves were huge, and more like miniature trees that what I'd been expecting. Each flower had a large trumpet-shaped base on top of stems that were thicker than my arm. The trumpets were almost a meter high, and the central stalks—what Bennet had called spathes—towered above them.

I glanced at the fountain, and saw the spathes reflected in the water's surface. Their reflections surrounded the moon's, like three daggers threatening to pierce the orb at any moment.

"Are the plants always arranged this way?" I asked. "Around the fountain like that?"

"No. They were rearranged when they started blooming, to make it easier for those who wished to study them," Bennet replied. "Is something wrong?"

"It looks like they're already set up for a ritual." I crouched down and moved aside one of the smaller potted palms, and saw that someone had made a circle around the corpse flowers and the fountain with gray stones that were a bit larger than the gravel, and smooth like river rock. As if that wasn't concerning enough, the larger stones had symbols etched into their surfaces.

"Who comes in here besides you?" I demanded as I pushed the larger rocks out of alignment, breaking the circle and hopefully whatever spell had been cast.

"Hundreds of people have access to this greenhouse," Bennet replied. "Thousands, if you take into account the entire student body and faculty." He paused. "Do you think this was a deliberate arrangement?"

"Yes." I held up one of the inscribed stones. "Have you noticed these larger stones?"

Bennet crouched down and picked one up. He frowned when he saw the symbol. "Eli, I had no idea—"

"I know you didn't. Let's just move them aside and see if that changes anything. Do you know what these symbols mean?"

"No, but I will research them." He glanced at me. "They do appear to be black magic."

I sighed. "Of course they do."

While Bennet and I grabbed the inscribed stones and tossed them aside, Nicholas walked up behind us.

"What's going on here?" he asked.

"Someone arranged these plants in such a way that they could possibly summon a spirit, demonic or otherwise," I replied without looking up. I hoped he'd assume I was crazy and leave us alone. No such luck.

"Ah. Is there anything I can do to assist?"

I looked up at him. "You believe me?"

"Why shouldn't I?" Nicholas countered. "Dr. Carrington, should you really be down on all fours like that?"

"Someone brought black magic into this glass house," he snapped. "I'll be damned if I let it stay here."

Nicholas cocked his head toward me. "Why do we think black magic is present?"

I handed him one of the stones, and explained, "The symbols on these rocks, and the way everything's been arranged around the fountain, is indicative of a summoning ritual. Bennet recognized the symbols as possible black magic."

"We've set everything up in this house according to the original plans. Would you like help removing the ones with symbols?"

"Sure."

Nicholas knelt down and started picking through the rocks. Since it was dark, and the river rocks were only a bit larger and darker than the surrounding gravel, it wasn't easy to find them. "The original did not have a display of corpse flowers, though."

"You mentioned plans. Was there a greenhouse here before this one?"

"No, not here at the college. I meant the plans from when this greenhouse was first erected," Nicholas replied. "This is an antique structure, and was shipped over from England, piece by piece. Dr. Carrington was quite pleased to acquire a classic house in such good repair."

"Huh." I grabbed a few more inscribed stones and threw them behind a potted banana tree. "Any idea where this greenhouse was situated in England?"

"It was on one of the properties owned by Sir Edmund Allwood in the seventeenth century."

"Allwood." I looked at him over my shoulder, then I went back to sorting rocks. "Any relation to your family?"

"The name should sound familiar, if you know your local history. The Allwoods were a one of the founding families of this area. Most claim they were the most powerful witch clan in the new world."

It was dark, and I wasn't facing Nicholas, so he didn't see me almost choke when he said that. Officially, witches didn't exist in the old or new worlds. Unofficially, old world practitioners of black magic were known around the globe for their intricate rituals and legendary clan wars. I could only imagine what these walls had witnessed over the centuries. And Bennet had hauled all that bad juju across the pond and plopped it right here in my backyard.

I realized that Nicholas hadn't answered my question. "Are you descended from those local Allwoods?"

"Me? Oh, no, not directly. My immediate family hails from England."

That was a relief. "Most think all that black magic stuff is just a bunch of rumors," I ventured. "Trying to be scandalous and all."

"Those have done their research know better," Nicholas said.

"For a gardener you're rather blasé about spirits and witches and such," I said.

"It pays to be familiar with occult history, especially in my profession. Why, tomatoes were once blamed for all sorts of supernatural occurrences, even lycanthropy."

I looked up at Nicholas and blew a lock of hair away from my nose. "Really?"

Lightning flashed, then the glass panes that made up the greenhouse shattered. I covered my head with my arms as shards flew toward us from the ceiling and walls. With the glass came a torrent of rain, as if a monsoon had set up shop directly above us. There was a horrible shrieking sound, like metal being torn apart.

Dr. Carrington had been correct: the corpse flowers had summoned an otherworldly force. And now it was here.

The noise and falling glass ended as abruptly as it had begun. I peeked around my arms, already stiff in my rainwater-soaked clothes. I looked upward, but I couldn't see a single cloud in the night sky. How had the rain started, and then ended, so abruptly?

"Eli," Bennet called. "Eliza, where are you?"

"I'm okay," I said as pushed myself upright. "You?"

"I'm bit scratched up, but the tweed held off the worst of it," he replied. "Nicholas? Nicholas, are you all right?"

I heard gravel crunching, and saw Nicholas raise himself up from behind the fountain. "It's dry," he said.

"What do you mean?" I asked. "Everything's wet."

"The fountain," he replied without looking at me. I followed his gaze, and saw that the fountain's basin was indeed dry as a bone. The three corpse flowers that surrounded it had been burnt to a crisp.

Chapter 2

Never Purchase Items From A Cursed Plot

I don't know who called the ambulance. It wasn't me, and I didn't see Bennet or Nicholas reach for a phone while broken glass and wind and rain swirled around us like a tornado of doom. While the three of us picked glass out of our hair, some well-meaning person had noticed the ruckus at the greenhouse, and called for help. As much as I would have preferred the authorities stay out of this situation, I appreciated those good Samaritans, whoever they were.

Along with the ambulance came the campus police, and then the real police, and finally the detectives arrived on the scene. After the first responders had sorted us out, I ended up sitting on an ambulance's rear bumper, with one of those reflective thermal blankets wrapped around my shoulders. The EMTs had left me there while they finished up with Bennet, who was inside the other ambulance having his left arm bandaged; they didn't think it was broken, but he had some deep lacerations on his forearm. I'd only sustained a few shallow scratches and bruises during that freak thunderstorm, which was what Bennet, Nicholas, and I had all agreed to tell the authorities: it was a weather event, no more, no less. Not a single person had believed that story, which meant that my least favorite law enforcement official, Detective Lyons, got to interview me about what had really gone down inside the greenhouse.

"And you're sure that you didn't see anything unusual before the ceiling shattered?" Detective Lyons asked me.

"I sure as hell didn't see anything that made me think it would shatter," I snapped. The antiseptic the EMTs had used to clean my wounds burned, my clothes were damp and smeared with dirt and crushed plant life, and Detective Lyons seemed like the ideal target for my foul mood.

"Why were you here after hours?" Detective Lyons asked. "You don't seem like the gardening type." He gave my leather jacket some side eye, and added, "You look like a biker in that."

"Funny. Maybe I'm a student."

"I checked the roster. You're not."

Of course, he'd checked the roster. "Dr. Carrington was a friend of my grandmother's," I replied. "He called me earlier and asked me to come down. He's really proud of his new greenhouse. It's an antique." And that was the truth.

Detective Lyons glanced over his shoulder at the ruined greenhouse. "It's a death trap, is what it is. Maybe the ceiling was installed wrong?"

"Great theory, Detective. Shoddy workmanship is obviously to blame for this debacle. I feel much better knowing that officers like you are looking out for my safety."

He gave me a look, his brows raised just enough to convey that he wasn't buying what I was selling. I probably should have used smaller words. Then he frowned, grabbed a handkerchief from his pocket and started dabbing at the skin near my temple.

"You sure they got all the glass out of your hair?" he asked. "You're still bleeding."

"I'm fine." I pushed his hand away and stood up, nearly bumping into him in the process. Then I tried walking away from him, but he grabbed my forearm.

"Listen, you and I both know something weird happened here," he said. "And I really don't think lightning struck the same spot three times and fried those plants."

"That's what—"

He held up a hand. "I may be a dumb cop, but I know how lightning works. Whatever happened here was the kind of weird that follows you everywhere. When you want to talk about it, call me."

I'd never been that close to Detective Lyons before. Ever since we'd first met, when he'd taken my statement about the belladonna incident at Forge Heights, I'd done everything I could to avoid him and his way too on the nose questions. Now, I couldn't move away. There was something about his deep brown eyes and square, stubbly jaw that was interesting. Compelling, even. Right then, they were compelling me to tell him things that could get both of us a lifetime pass to the looney bin. Has he always smelled this good?

"If I remember anything else that I think might help your investigation, I'll call you," I said. "Promise."

He squeezed my arm. "See that you do."

I shook my arm free from his grasp, and walked away from the flashing blue and red police lights. What I needed to do was get someplace quiet, sit down, and think about what had happened here. I needed to figure out a plan, and I needed to know what sort of entity had fried those plants, and where it was going. Before any of that happened I needed a shower, a snack, and twelve hours of sleep.

"Miss Moore."

I turned toward the voice, and saw Nicholas melt out of the shadows. He'd gotten cut up much more than I had, and the dried blood on his forehead made his hair seem black in the darkness. "Hey. Do they want to take you to the hospital?"

"They suggested it, but I declined," he replied. "I would prefer to get a jump on our research."

"Research?"

"Yes. I have a rather extensive library at home, and Dr. Carrington has asked me to get started on this current problem as soon as possible. We do need answers rather quickly, I'd say."

"We? There is no we here. Bennet asked me to come down to look at some weird flowers. I did, and it was a bad decision on my part. My involvement is over."

"Miss Moore, you cannot just let than entity run amok," Nicholas said, loudly enough to make Detective Lyons and the rest of the emergency responders stop what they were doing and watch us. Attention from them was exactly what I didn't need, and I didn't need Nicholas's attention, either.

"You cannot just walk away," Nicholas continued.

"Watch me."

I turned on my heel and walked away from the ruined greenhouse and the dozen emergency vehicles, away from Bennet and Nicholas and Detective Lyons and all of the rumors that were already swirling around this incident. I didn't stop walking until I reached my car, and kept my mind carefully blank as I drove home. Once I was inside my apartment I closed and locked the door, leaned back against the wood and took a deep breath. Then I slid down to the floor, drew my knees up to my chest, and finally let myself exhale.

What the hell had I gotten myself into?

***

Demons and ghosts had always been part of my life, even before Gran had told me about our family's history. Until I was eight I'd had a relatively ordinary childhood. Back then I still lived with my disinterested but perfectly adequate mother. Luckily for the world at large she'd only reproduced once, as far as I know, thus sparing any potential siblings from endless boredom while she ignored us. She always made sure I was fed, and bathed, and had good clothes for school, but anything other than basic child maintenance was beyond her.

When I was in the third grade my mother signed me up for one of those weekly troop meeting groups. It was like a low-rent version of the Girl Scouts where I got to socialize outside of the classroom with kids my own age, with the bonus that Mom got rid of me in a safe and legal manner for a few hours every Tuesday afternoon. That made it a win for both of us.

The group met in the basement of an old school. Classes were no longer taught there, and the building had been transitioned into a community center. We gathered in the repurposed gymnasium and worked on arts and crafts, always leaving behind a layer of glue and glitter on the shiny wood floor for the cleaning staff to deal with in the morning. During one meeting at the end of March we were excited for spring, and the craft du jour was tissue paper flowers. One of my troop mates, Jada, had gotten bored with making flowers and went snooping in the old coat room. After a few minutes she emerged with an antique mirror that looked like it had once graced a Victorian lady's dressing table.

"We should decorate it," Jada squealed, after she'd dragged it over to our table. Behind her was a thick groove dug into the wood floor, courtesy of the mirror's sharp corner.

"We can do that," said the group's token adult leader, Becky, as she leapt forward to catch the mirror before it fell over and shattered. "Let's put the flowers around the edge and make it look like a fairy pond."

While Becky positioned the mirror on the floor in the center of the room, we gathered up our half-crushed paper flowers and taped them to the edges of our makeshift pond. It wasn't long before our fairy pond was complete and we gathered around it, gazing at our creation. The glass was so old it was warped, and our wavy reflections made it seem like we really were looking into water.

"The mirror is like a doorway," Jada mumbled.

"What's that?" Becky asked.

"We can see ourselves, but not the regular versions," Jada explained. "All we can see is our backward selves. Like copies."

"Are the fairies backwards versions of people?" another girl asked.

"I don't know," Becky said. "But if I ever meet a fairy I'll be sure to ask."

"Can they come through?" I asked. "The fairies, I mean. Can we call them?"

"If anything did come through it would be very bad," Jada warned, then the lights went out.

"Everyone stay calm," Becky said. "I'm sure the power will be back on in a minute."

I heard rustling, and at first assumed it was some old trash or leaves being blown around by the March wind. Then I realized that the sound wasn't coming from outside the school. It was emanating from the center of our fairy mirror.

"Where did you get this mirror?" I whispered to Jada. "Why is it making noise? Mirrors don't do that."

"Don't they?"

That voice hadn't been Jada's little-girl lilt. It had sounded like an old man, an old mean man that didn't belong anywhere near a group of third-grade girls. I turned toward Jada and saw her grinning like a feral beast, her eyes flashing red and orange.

The next thing I remembered was waking up in the hospital. After I told the doctors what I'd seen in Jada's face they transferred me to a stark white room on a special floor. Later, I was told that after the lights went out I'd gone hysterical and fainted, which I'd thought was a good response based on the fact that the girl standing next to me had had flames dancing in her eyes. I was stuck in that room, undergoing one boring test after the next, until my grandmother rescued me and I went to live with her.

I never saw my mother, or Jada, again.

***

As I sat on my cold apartment floor I thought about that day with the fairy mirror. It had happened twenty years ago, and we'd been making spring flowers because the next day was April first. April Fools' Day. Bennet had mentioned that the corpse flowers blooming so close to April Fools' Day was dire...

I got up off the floor, set my phone on the bookcase by the door, and peeled off my bloody, dusty clothes as I walked toward the bathroom. My apartment had two entrances: the front door, which opened into the waiting room and office for Nine Lives Investigations, and was used by potential clients. I'd entered through the back door, to which only Tessa and I had a key. The back entrance was my favorite, since it was free from prying eyes and inquisitive customers. Tonight I was extra grateful for that back door, since my trail of destroyed clothes could scare off most of my clientele. I'd had too much experience with those who wouldn't run at the sight of a blood-spattered wardrobe. Working with those sorts never ends well, least of all for me.

I stepped into the shower and cranked up the heat as high as it would go. After the scalding water rinsed off the last of the dust and debris from the greenhouse, I toweled off, put on my bathrobe and went into the kitchen. I was staring into the refrigerator when the office line rang.

"Nine Lives," I said when I picked up. "We're closed right now, but I can take a message."

"It's Bennet," came his tired voice. "Are you all right?"

"Yeah. How's your arm?"

"Sore. This will definitely hamper my Jiu Jitsu training." He paused, and I wondered if he was serious. The idea of Bennet Carrington doing backflips in a dojo almost made me smile. "After the police and the rest left the school I went back into the greenhouse for another look around. I pocketed a few of those inscribed stones, and I intend to attempt a translation of the symbols."

"Won't that be difficult?"

"Oh, yes. Most likely." Bennet paused. "Did you hear anything? Just as the lightning struck."

"Other than crashing glass? No."

"It could be my mind playing tricks on me, but I could swear I heard a name. Nathaniel."

"Nathaniel," I repeated, drawing out the syllables. "Is that an entity? One that might be responsible for all of this?"

"That I do not know yet."

"I'll help you research this Nathaniel, or whatever its name is," I said. "I'll even help you get rid of it, if we can."

"Thank you, Eli. That means a lot to me."

When he paused, I said, "I'm sorry about your greenhouse. It was really nice."

"Yes, well, I suppose that's what one gets for purchasing items from a cursed plot. Get some rest, Eli."

"You, too."

I set down the phone, then I sat behind my desk and grabbed a notepad. I wrote down Nathaniel, first in cursive and then printed, and stared at the name for a few moments. I was certain I'd never met anyone with that name, and no one named Nathaniel had ever come by Gran's while I was around. I wondered if this could be someone left over from Gran's spirit hunting heyday, and if we were really dealing with a demon, or just a self-important ghost. Since sleep seemed out of the question, I decided to start my own research right away.

I filled the electric kettle and set it to boil, and then I rummaged around in the cabinets for something crunchy. All I found was a bag of rice cakes, but they were fresh so they won the snack game. I'd just powered up my laptop when the kettle whistled. A few minutes later I sat down with my rice cakes and a cup of tea, and typed Nathaniel into my browser's search field. Wow, that returned a lot of hits.

I clicked around the internet for hours, looking for connections between people named Nathaniel, corpse flowers, and supernatural phenomenon. I even read a rather in-depth history of Sir Edmund Allwood and the property the greenhouse had originally sat on, and I learned what kind of education was needed to work in horticulture. None of those subjects were connected, not even peripherally, and I found absolutely no mention of someone named Nathaniel linked to any of those subjects, either as a demon, place, or person. Frustrated and exhausted, I shut my laptop and went to bed.

CHAPTER 3

DON'T LEAVE HOME WITHOUT YOUR WITCHFINDER

I WOKE UP WHEN I heard the apartment's front door click open. I sat straight up in bed, cold sweat blooming across my shoulders.

No. Not again.

I took a breath and centered myself, then I felt underneath the mattress for the knife I kept there. It was an old kitchen knife and was desperately in need of sharpening, but it was big and looked menacing. I hoped.

"Eli?" Tessa called.

I let out a sigh of relief and lowered the knife. "Be right out."

I put on some jeans and a long-sleeved knit shirt, then I exited my bedroom. I found Tessa standing in my office, shaking her head. There were bits of rice cake scattered across my desk, and I'd never picked up my clothes after I'd showered. I'd also left a path of muddy footsteps across the hardwood floor, complete with crumpled up leaves. The place looked like I'd decorated for Halloween six months ahead of time.

"What's up?" I asked. "You specifically don't work on Saturdays."

She picked up my leather jacket and hung it on its designated peg. "I saw the news."

I sat on the leather couch I kept for clients. It was the nicest piece of furniture I owned. "It was on the news?"

"It was the featured story. In my youth, if something like that happened, we would arm the townspeople with pitchforks and torches and send them searching door to door for witches."

"Luckily, those days are behind us." When Tessa remained silent, I asked, "Aren't they?"

Tessa sat next to me and patted my hand. "Can you tell me what happened?"

I told Tessa everything that went down the night before, beginning with Nicholas Allwood letting me into the greenhouse and ending with my late night research and snacking binge.

"So, after the thunder and the raining glass and all, the corpse plants were just incinerated?" Tessa asked.

"They weren't exactly incinerated," I replied. "They were still upright in their pots, with those long center stalks sticking up. But they'd been burnt so badly all three of them were charred black."

"Did lightning really strike all three of them?"

"No. We just told the cops that because it made more sense than us getting attacked by spirits." I rubbed the back of my neck. "Honestly, I guess it could have been lightning. I don't remember much of anything after the glass came down."

"What did the ghost feel like?" Tessa asked.

"I... You know, I don't remember sensing a ghost, or any other kind of spirit." I sat back as I played back last night's events in my mind's eye. I'd experienced the gamut of emotions in that greenhouse, but I hadn't felt a single entity. Non-sensitives assume that all old buildings are teeming with ghosts, but that's just the arrogance of the living. Most people move on to whatever plane they're destined for once they pass. It was the rare soul with a mission—or one holding an especially mean grudge—that stayed behind. My grandmother, who was one of the most powerful seers of the last hundred years, had only visited me once after she'd passed, and that was just to let me know she was all right. Gran wouldn't be making any more unscheduled appearances unless the shit really hit the fan.

The ghost who'd helped me find Abigail Stevens had had a mission: to never let any child be hurt the way hers were, not ever again. So far she was doing a great job.

"Huh," Tessa said. "There must have been some kind of spirit involved. I don't think any of that could be attributed to a lighting storm."

I gave her a look. "Now you sound like Detective Lyons."

"He has it bad for you," Tessa said.

"He does not!"

"He shows up at every single weird case that gets called in, just hoping you'll be there."

"I am at all the weird cases," I reminded her. "And honestly, this is getting to be a problem. The way he was questioning me last night I thought he wanted to bring me down to the station. What would I do then, lie under oath?"

"Do they make you take an oath when you're being questioned?" Tessa mused. "How can they even enforce that?"

"I have no idea, but he made me promise to call him if I remembered anything else."

"Maybe you should call him, and let him take you out for coffee."

"Tess!"

She laughed, then she got up and surveyed the office. "Fine, be a spinster. Since I'm already here, let's get this place cleaned up so we don't scare off the paying customers on Monday." She nudged my torn and filthy jeans, still on the floor where I'd dropped them, with the toe of her boot. "We might have to burn this."

"Agreed. Usual overtime arrangement?"

"I'll start cleaning, you get the coffee and bagels."

"Deal."

***

I'd just gotten back to the office with our breakfast when my cell buzzed in my back pocket. I fished it out, and accepted the call. "Hello?"

"Miss Moore, this is Nicholas Allwood," came the crisp reply. I didn't remember giving Nicholas my cell number, but I figured he'd gotten it from Bennet.

"Good morning. What can I do for you?"

"Dr. Carrington had asked me to research Indonesian demons, and I've come across a few things you might be interested in."

"Why Indonesian demons?"

"Amorphophallus titanium is endemic to that region," Nicholas replied. Before I asked how he knew that, I remembered. Horticulturist. "Dr. Carrington believed that a specific entity may be historically associated with its native habitat, therefore we would have a blueprint on how to contain it."

"Did you find anything about a Nathaniel?"

Nicholas paused, then asked, "Where did you hear that name?"

"Bennet called last night. He mentioned the name Nathaniel. I figured he told you, too."

"He did." Nicholas cleared his throat, and continued, "Miss Moore, I do not know how secure this line may be. Are you able to join me at my home?"

"Have you told Bennet what you found?" I countered. "Maybe we can both meet him at the college."

"I have indeed informed him, and he will be here directly," Nicholas replied. "He was hoping you would join us."

"All right," I replied, then Nicholas gave me his address. We ended the call, then I set down the paper bags and cup carrier and went in search of Tessa. I found her watering my potted belladonna.

"Are you sure this is a good idea?" Tess asked after I explained where I was going. "You of all people should know better than to go to an unknown house by yourself. Want me to come with you?"

"No," I snapped, irritated that Tessa still thought of me as a whimpering teen that needed to be saved. Tessa frowned, then she pulled me into a hug.

"I get it. I really do," she said. "And I don't think you should be going to that man's house alone. He could be a serial killer."

"You wouldn't say that if you'd ever seen Nicholas," I said. When she didn't let up, I added, "He's about as threatening as a blueberry muffin. Besides, Bennet will be there, too."

"I suppose having Bennet present is better than nothing." She released me and gave my outfit a once over. Tessa frequently bemoaned my go-to choices of tee shirt, jeans, boots, and leather jacket. "Please tell me you're at least bringing your witchfinder."

I patted my jacket pocket. "Never leave home without it."

"I do wish you'd wear it, but having it in your pocket is better than nothing." Tessa grabbed a notepad and a pen from the desk, and set them down in front of me. "You are going to humor me and write down Nicholas's address and phone number. Email, too, if you have it." She fluttered her eyelashes and added, "If you don't come home I'll need to tell Officer Muscleman where he can find your body."

"Who—do you mean Detective Lyons?"

"Who else?"

I grimaced, then I wrote down Nicholas's phone number and address. "You need to stop calling him Officer Muscleman. If he finds out about that nickname we'll never get rid of him."

Tessa smiled. "That's the idea."

"You're awful." I grabbed my keys, and said, "I'll call you when I'm on my way back." With that, I left my office and Tessa's ridiculous ideas behind.

CHAPTER 4

SHE'S MY SISTER

NICHOLAS'S HOME WAS A townhouse in one of the newly gentrified neighborhoods on the south side of town, which meant that the place was tiny and the rent was probably astronomical. Maybe being an assistant horticulturist paid well. I wondered how much Bennet was getting paid. Probably a lot, if he could afford to purchase antique greenhouses and have them shipped all the way from England.

I really hoped he'd taken out insurance on that greenhouse.

I walked up the townhouse's concrete steps, rang the bell, and waited. Less than a minute later, a charming and attractive blond man opened the door. He was dressed casually but not sloppily, in khaki pants and a dark green wool sweater over a checkered button-down shirt. The only aspect of his appearance that reminded me of the haughty man I'd met the day before were his wire-rimmed glasses.

"Miss Moore," Nicholas said. "I'm delighted that you came by."

"Nicholas?" I asked. "I almost didn't recognize you. You look so... Relaxed."

He blushed and ducked his head. A shock of blond hair fell over his eyes and made him even more adorable. "Forgive me. Last night was certainly eventful, and I do tend to get a bit stiff under stress."

I bit the inside of my cheek and tamped down all the naughty comebacks fighting for release. "Yeah, last night was one for the record books."

"It certainly was." He glanced up and our gazes met, and for a moment I was actually lost in his eyes. If this moment got any cheesier I'd have to change my middle name from Jayne to Gouda.

"You said you found some information about our common problem," I said.

Nicholas blushed again. "Yes. Forgive me, where are my manners? This way, Miss Moore."

Nicholas stepped aside and swept his arm toward the interior of the townhouse. Once my eyes adjusted to the dimly lit foyer, I realized his home was decorated like a jazz era Park Avenue hotel, complete with a crystal chandelier, ruby toned damask wallpaper, and dark wood paneling.

"Do you own this place?" I asked. When he cocked an eyebrow, I elaborated, "Most rentals I've been inside aren't quite this opulent."

"I understand what you mean; rentals do tend to be rather boring. And yes, my sister and I are the owners of this property. An ancestor of ours left it to us. She immigrated here from the old country some time ago, and this home has been in our family ever since." He nodded toward the brass umbrella stand and grimaced. "As you can see, we've not gotten 'round to redecorating."

"I like it. It's a rich look, historical even."

"Thank you. May I take your coat?"

"Um, sure." I shrugged out of my jacket and handed it over. While Nicholas hung it on the coat rack, I looked down the hallway toward the one area that wasn't dark and dreary. "Is that your kitchen?"

"Yes. Would you join me for some tea?"

"I like tea."

Nicholas motioned for me to follow him, and he led me into a happy, light-filled kitchen. While he busied himself with making our tea, I checked out the surroundings. The countertops were white marble and the cabinets were pale wood, and there were lots of green leafy plants crammed onto the shelves and hanging from the ceiling in lovely macramé hangers.

Call me nosy—occupational hazard, you know—but the two best ways of learning about a person were by rifling through their trash and seeing what they kept within easy reach. Since going through Nicholas's wastebasket wasn't an option at the moment, I sidled over to the fridge. There weren't any takeout menus attached to the front of it, which made me wonder if he—or his sister—cooked. I liked men that cooked.

While there were no pizza or Thai menus on hand, the refrigerator door was far from bare. There was a calendar with past dates crossed off, a flyer from a green grocer, and a lone photograph in a cute magnetic frame. It had been taken outdoors in autumn, and was of Nicholas and a woman.

"Is this your girlfriend?" I asked.

He laughed. "Not hardly. That's my sister, Jada."

"Jada?" I repeated. "I used to know a Jada." I leaned closer to the picture, examining Nicholas's sister. She was as dark as he was light, with nearly black hair and eyes... and she looked like an adult version of the Jada I'd known back in the third grade. "When did you say you inherited this place?"

Pain exploded across the base of my skull. The world went red, then black.

CHAPTER 5

POSSESSED, LIKE IN A HORROR MOVIE

WHEN I CAME TO, I was tied to a chair. I was also bent forward with my throbbing head resting on the kitchen table. I opened my eyes, then immediately squeezed them shut as the afternoon sun sent daggers shooting into my brain. What had been a happy room filled with sunshine was now actively conspiring against me.

"Ow." I tried to rub the sore spot on the back of my skull against my shoulder, and you can imagine how well that worked out.

"Aww, does it hurt?" a woman's voice asked. I managed to sit up and saw a dark-haired woman standing over me. My senses cleared a bit more, and I realized she was the woman from the picture on the fridge. Nicholas's sister. Jada.

"Did I fall?" I asked. I knew damn well I hadn't fallen, but I hoped that if I played dumb, she would to relax her guard and start talking.

"You, fall?" she sneered. "The righteous Eliza Moore, champion of do-gooders everywhere? If anything, you can fly."

"Ah, I think you're talking about a different Eliza," I said. "I'm not the champion of anything, and I'm very clumsy. I've got two left feet, really. I can't even dance. Once, in middle school—"

Jada slapped me across the mouth. Her ring caught my lip and tore it open. My eyes welled up as the side of my mouth burned in pain.

"Shut up," Jada said. "I don't need you mucking things up."

I nodded, doing my best to look wide-eyed and terrified as blood dribbled down my chin. Jada scowled at me, then she looked past me as Nicholas entered the kitchen carrying a brown paper grocery bag. He glanced at me and his brows pinched, then he walked to the far side of the room.

"About time," Jada snapped. "Do you have everything?"

"I believe so," he replied. Based on the soft thud behind me, I assumed he set the bag on the counter. "And the digitalis has dried out nicely."

Digitalis? I peeked over my shoulder and saw Nicholas pulling down a bunch of dried stalks from one of the shelves. They'd been bundled together and hung upside down from the ceiling, just like how my gran used to dry herbs. I wracked my sore brain, trying to remember what digitalis was used for.

"Are you going to kill me?" I blurted out when I remembered that digitalis—also known as foxglove—could send a person into cardiac arrest.

"Not completely," Jada said. "We just need to stop your heart long enough for me to jump from this body into yours."

There was the bit of information I needed. Jada had a spirit—most likely the Nathaniel entity from the greenhouse—controlling her body. "That's not how possessions work," I said

"It's how this possession works." Jada crouched down in front of me, and I saw the same orange and red flames dancing in her eyes that I remembered from the school gymnasium twenty years ago. "Way back when you were a snot nosed brat, you released me from the mirror that was my prison. When I broke free little Jada got so scared her heart stopped, and that's how I got in."

I felt the blood drain from my face. "You've been riding her all these years?"

"Yes, and it is awful," Jada spat. "Do you know how limited I am by this meat sack? I can barely control another human." She glared at Nicholas. He frowned, picked up the bundle of herbs, and left the room.

I jerked my chin toward the door Nicholas had gone through. "Is he really Jada's brother?"

"Does it matter?" she countered. "I'm ready to be rid of these two. Fighting with the child to control this form is not how I wish to spend my days."

Whenever you think things can't get any worse, the Powers That Be inevitably take it up a notch. "Is Jada still... in there?"

The demon with Jada's face smiled. "Perhaps she is. Want to slice me open and have a look?"

There was a noise in another room, which I hoped had been made by Nicholas and not some other possessed human, or worse. Without a word Jada left the room. Once I was alone in the kitchen, I took a few deep breaths and centered myself by concentrating on physical sensations. It was a trick I'd learned in my late teens, and it hadn't failed me yet. I focused on the feel of the rope around my wrists, the hard wooden chair beneath me, and the faint scent of chamomile in the air. Thus calmed, I reached out with my senses and confirmed that whatever was riding Jada was the only entity in the house. I guessed that was good, since exorcising that spirit should help both Jada and Nicholas.

There was a scratching sound behind me. Great, I was tied up in a kitchen that had rats. The scratching became rattling, then the window over the sink slid open. My jaw nearly hit the floor as I watched Detective Lyons climb in through the window. He held his finger to his lips, then he clambered off the counter and skulked toward me.

"What are you doing here?" I hissed. "Were you following me?"

"I knew you weren't telling me everything last night," he hissed back. "Who taught you to lie to the cops?"

"Stalker."

"Captive."

Never in my life had I wanted to smack anyone as much as I wanted to smack him. "Detective Lyons—"

"I'm off duty. Call me Dan." He got up and did a quick circuit of the room, then he darted out into the hallway. When he came back into the kitchen he knelt behind me and jerked my bound hands toward him. It only took him a moment to untie the ropes, and I was free.

"Thanks," I said as I rubbed my wrists.

"Don't mention it." His gaze focused on my mouth. "You're bleeding."

"I'll be fine."

He nodded. "Let's get out of here." He stood, but I grabbed his arm.

"I can't leave," I said. "Did you see the woman, Jada? She's my friend. Well, she was, but now she's possessed."

"Possessed? Like in a horror movie?"

"Yeah." I held his gaze, and continued, "Listen, this is the most straight I've ever been with you. Jada is in trouble, and she needs our help."

Dan frowned. "What about the guy from the college? He her pimp or something?"

"He's her brother." I heard footsteps in the hallway. "Hide!"

"We need to get out of here," Dan said, but I shook my head.

"Dan, please. They need our help."

Dan gave me a look that could have stopped a clock, then he slipped inside the pantry and closed the door. A bare second later Nicholas reentered the room.

"I just want to know one thing," I said without preamble. "What did corpse flowers have to do with all of this?"

"Oh, the corpse flowers were only for show. We needed a way for you and me to meet," Nicholas replied. "Our initial plan was to have Jada reenter your life, but the spirit possessing her might have given everything away. We couldn't have you suspecting something out of the ordinary."

"Is the spirit Nathaniel?"

Nicholas cocked his head to the side. "I can confirm his involvement."

Getting confirmation that the mysterious Nathaniel was the big bad was not at all satisfying. "You learned all about gardening to get a job with Bennet? That's impressive."

"No. I faked my credentials and got a job with Dr. Carrington. Then we arranged the greenhouse with spelled stones that coaxed all of the corpse flowers to bloom all at once, knowing that Dr. Carrington wouldn't be able to overlook such an anomaly." Nick faced me. "We—the spirit and I—have been watching you for years. Dr. Carrington is one of the few people you never cut ties with after your grandmother died. Why is that, I wonder?"

I glanced at the pantry. Dan was watching us through the barely open door, but that was all he was doing. "How much did you learn about Dr. Carrington?" I asked, desperate to keep Nicholas distracted.

"Enough to wonder what that doddering old fool was really up to. As it turns out he has a network of ladies all across the globe he regularly corresponds with. Are you all seers, or is he just drawn to the young and foolish ones?" Nicholas came around the table and stopped short. "How did you untie yourself?"

Crap, my hands were in my lap. "The rope fell off. Weird, huh?"

Nick took a step toward me. Out of the corner of my eye I saw Dan ease the pantry door open a bit farther. "How stupid do you think I am, Miss Moore?"

I swallowed hard. "Is that a rhetorical question?"

Dan grabbed a coffee mug from the counter and moved to strike Nicholas. Without turning around Nicholas's arm shot out, and he punched Dan in the face so hard he dropped to the floor.

"No, it was not." Nicholas opened a drawer and withdrew a burlap sack.

"No, wait," I said and he put the sack over my head and held it around my neck. The rough fabric scratched my face and caught my hair. After a few breaths I felt dizzy, and there was a sweet taste in the back of my mouth; chloroform. Goddammit, Nicholas was knocking me out. Soon enough, the world was black again.

***

When I came to the second time, the sack wasn't on my head. I sucked in big gulps of air, thrilled that I could breathe without the rough, damp fabric against my face. After I'd made myself dizzy with all that oxygen, I realized my hands were tied behind my back. This was getting old.

Speaking of my back, mine was leaning against someone's, and their wrists were bound to mine. For the first time since we'd met, I hoped Detective Lyons was right behind me.

"Hey," I whispered over my shoulder. "Dan?"

"Ain't Santa Claus," he rasped. I wondered if Nicholas had drugged Dan, too. "Where are we?"

"I don't know." The room was so dark I couldn't differentiate the walls from the floor or the ceiling. The only facts I could glean from our surroundings was that it was cold, and we were sitting on a hard floor. "Basement?"

I felt his hands reach toward the floor. "Floor's wood, so we're probably not in the basement."

"Is that good?"

He shrugged. "No idea." Dan turned his head until his mouth was close to my ear. "Just sit tight. Shouldn't be too much longer till they get here."

"Who? Jada the Death Witch and her lackey brother?"

His shoulders shook. Here we were, tied up in a house with a crazy possessed woman, and he was laughing at me. "You're funny, you know that? After Tessa called me with this address, I called it in to the station. I told them if I didn't check in in an hour to come after us."

"Tessa told you where I was going?"

"Tessa is the only one with her head on straight around here," Dan said. "What were you thinking, coming out here alone? She was scared for you. And she was right," he added.

"Tessa's always right," I said, and then, because of that earlier lack of oxygen to my brain, I added, "She said we should go out. Not out out, but for something like coffee."

Dan went still. "I like coffee."

I angled my head until I could almost see him over my shoulder. "Yeah?"

The overhead lights switched on, and I squeezed my eyes shut. This house had two ambient light settings, either pitch black or so bright it scorched your retinas.

Jada and Nicholas were moving around the perimeter of the room, speaking in low tones. Dan grabbed a few of my fingers and squeezed.

I realized that the way our wrists had been tied meant that his hands were pressed against my lower back, right above my belt.

"My jeans," I whispered. "Inside the waist."

I felt his fingertips lift up my shirt and move against my skin, making every hair on my body stand on end. He felt along the inside of my waistband, halting when he felt the tiny pocket sewn into the denim. It was a rectangle of cheap rayon, and inside it was a razor blade.

Dan freed the blade and started sawing at our bonds. The razor nicked my wrist, but I bit the inside of my mouth and stayed silent. While I thought about anything but the pain, I looked around the room and saw a man's body crumpled in a corner. I couldn't see his face, but I recognized that tweed waistcoat.

"Bennet," I said. Jada and Nicholas stopped what they were doing and moved toward me. Dan stopped sawing at the ropes, and laced the fingers of his free hand with mine. "Is he dead?"

"Not yet," Jada replied. "Perhaps we won't kill him at all. Since he knows so many, many seers, I think he could be quite useful. However, we do need some blood for the ritual. Good thing your friend failed at rescuing you."

"Take mine instead," I said. Dan started saying something, but I spoke over him. "Come on, you said you need me near death. Use my blood, but leave Dan and Bennet alone."

"I don't need your blood," Jada said. "I only need your heart to stop."

Jada looked at Nicholas, and he approached me with an earthenware mug. I assumed they had steeped the dried digitalis into a tea, and that was how they would accomplish nearly killing and then having the entity leave Jada's body and possess me.

Well. You know what happens when you assume.

Nicholas crouched in front of me and held the mug near my mouth. "Drink."

I leaned forward, blinking my eyes at the steam. "It's too hot," I said. "Can you blow on it?"

"What?"

"You know, to cool it off. Like your mom did when you were a kid." My mother had never blown on hot tea or soup for me, but I figured that was the sort of nurturing thing that other mothers did for their children.

"Did she drink it?" Jada asked.

"She's about to," Nicholas replied. He frowned, then he brought the mug closer to his mouth and parted his lips to blow on the hot tea.

I felt the razor cut through the last of the rope that bound me to Dan.

Wide eyed, I watched Nicholas blow on the tea, then I launched myself forward and upended the mug onto his neck and chest.

Nicholas bellowed something fierce—that tea was really hot—and the two of us tumbled together in a heap. Behind me, Dan got to his feet and held out his hands.

"Listen, no one's gotten hurt yet." He glanced at Nicholas's steaming chest, and added, "Not bad, anyway. Everyone can still walk out of here."

"Can we?" Jada demanded. "Where will we go? What will you do with the little girl possessed by me, and the man that kept her hidden?"

"We'll get you some help," Dan replied.

"There is no help for me," Jada roared, her mouth opening wider than any mouth should, so wide I could see the inside of her throat. It was black and charred, just like the corpse flowers had been. "The only help I need is getting out of this body and into a new one!"

"Is there any more tea?" I whispered to Nicholas.

"Yes, about a quart," he replied. "Why?"

"Go get it. I'm going to get that thing out of Jada."

"You can't—"

"Don't you want your sister back? Don't you want your life back?" When he didn't answer, I continued, "Go, while she's distracted. Get the tea."

Nicholas nodded, then he slunk along the floor and out to the hallway. I looked at Jada, and saw the flames dancing in her eyes. That meant the entity was close to the surface, which was right where I wanted it.

Jada was prowling toward Dan with her back toward me. I reached under my pant leg and withdrew an extendable baton I kept strapped to my calf for emergencies. This qualified. I flicked the baton open as I rushed Jada and smacked her across the back of her head. She swayed once, and fell to the floor.

"Hold her down," I yelled, and Dan threw himself on top of Jada. Nathaniel may be a demon, but he was inhabiting a body that was much smaller, and evidently much weaker, than Dan's. Nicholas returned with the tea, and nearly fell over when he saw us.

"Nick, hold her legs," I said as I took the beaker of tea. "Dan, get in front of me. Sit on her arms and hold her head still."

They got into position as I straddled Jada's chest.

"I cast you out," I said. Jada spat in my face. "You've controlled Jada long enough. It's time for you to go."

"You cannot harm me without harming her," Jada-Nathaniel sneered. "You don't have the guts."

"Yeah?"

I rose up, then sat down hard on Jada's stomach. Her mouth opened wide as the air whooshed out of her, irritating Nathaniel and dazing the mortal woman. While she struggled to catch her breath I grabbed her jaw and poured the digitalis tea down Jada's throat.

"Out," I yelled as I held her mouth and nose closed, forcing her to swallow. "I cast you out, spirit that doesn't belong! Get out of this mortal form, now!"

Jada-Nathaniel's eyes flamed and she bit my fingers. I cried out, but I kept my hand in place until I saw her throat work. I withdrew my hand and shook it out, and saw my blood smeared across Jada's face.

"Don't worry, I won't bite you again," Jada-Nathaniel said. "I want my new body in good condition."

"I've got no vacancies," I said. Jada's face went ashen, a sign that the digitalis was doing its job. "Dan, Nick, cover your mouths."

I slapped both of my hands over my mouth as Jada's eyes rolled back in her head. Thick, greasy smoke poured out of her mouth and nose. It swirled around me, but I kept my hands in place and my head down. Crap, could Nathaniel get in through my ears?

Eventually the smoke congealed near the ceiling, then it dissipated altogether. Jada went limp under me. I kept my hands on my face for a count of thirty after the smoke was gone.

"Call 911." When neither Nicholas nor Dan moved, I repeated, "Call 911! She's gonna need medical!"

Nicholas jumped up and sprinted out of the room. I moved off Jada's torso as Dan leaned down and put his ear next to her mouth.

"Is she breathing?"

"Yeah. Shallow, but she's doing it."

I rubbed my eyes. "I can't believe that worked."

"She really was possessed," Dan mumbled. "As a cop I've seen a thousand crazy things, but I never thought this could be real."

"This?"

"Ghosts. Possession." Dan raised his head and met my gaze. "You."

A groan from the far side of the room interrupted what was becoming a very awkward moment. I went to Bennet's side and helped him sit up.

"Are you all right?" I asked. "Do you need a doctor?"

"I'll live." His gaze fell on Jada. "What happened to her?"

I gave him the abridged version, from the fairy mirror right up until Nathaniel billowed free from Jada's body. I'd just finished when we heard the sirens.

"I'll go talk to the boys in blue," Dan said. After he was gone Bennet touched my hand.

"Where did Nathaniel end up?"

"Nowhere," I replied. "He didn't slip into me or Dan or Nicholas, since our mouths were covered. He just floated away."

"Ah."

"What, ah? What are you thinking?"

"I am thinking that there is a rather put out entity on the loose."

CHAPTER 6

FIFTY-FOUR SUFFOLK STREET

"More tea?" Tessa asked.

"I'd love some."

Bennet held out his cup, and Tessa dutifully filled it. He'd come by my apartment-slash-office almost every day in the week since we'd rescued Jada, and Tessa just loved fussing over him. If it wasn't for their very large age gap, I'd say she had a crush on him.

Actually, age gaps didn't much bother Tessa.

"Tess, why don't you tell Bennet about the time Queen Elizabeth made witchcraft a felony," I suggested.

Bennet laughed, but Tessa didn't miss a beat. "I still can't believe she did that. It threw the entire court into an uproar, but her majesty did love drama."

Bennet set down his teacup. "Are you quite serious?"

The front door opened and closed, and after tossing a coy glance at Bennet, Tessa went out to greet whomever it was. "Eliza, you seem to be doing well," Bennet said.

"So do you." He claimed to have completely healed from his ordeal in the Allwoods' house, where he'd been lured in much like I was. As for me, my fingers were still bandaged and my mouth was a bit sore, but those wounds were healing as well. "Have you made any headway translating the symbols on the river rocks?"

"I have, but not the headway I would have preferred. I've come to the conclusion that the symbols are complete gibberish."

"Nick said the corpse flower routine was all a ruse to get me to the greenhouse," I said. "At least they're not demonic."

"Yes, there is that."

"Eli, you have a visitor," Tessa called.

"Excuse me," I said, then I walked past Tessa and her smug grin, and found Dan Lyons standing in my waiting room. He was dressed for work, complete with a bad suit and sporting his badge on his belt.

"Detective Lyons," I greeted.

He laughed and shook his head. "It's Dan to you." He paused, and added, "Eli."

I felt my cheeks warm. I hoped Dan didn't notice it. "How are Nick and Jada?"

"Slightly better, and not great," he replied. "The DA's decided against prosecuting Nick, since there's no evidence of wrongdoing."

"That's good." After the police arrived at Nicholas's, they took in the trashed house and battered, disoriented Jada, and someone got the bright idea that Nick had been holding her captive. In reality, it had been the other way around. "And Jada?"

"She still thinks she's an eight-year-old girl. She has no memory of the past twenty years. Near as the doctors can tell, she's had a psychotic break." Dan paused, and added, "But that's not what happened."

"What do you think happened?"

"Honestly, I've got no idea," he replied. "All I know is one thing."

"And what's that?"

"I'm going to take you up on that coffee date."

"Sounds good. Wait, it will not be a date!"

Dan's face stretched into a lazy, half-lidded grin. "Whatever you say."

Laughter floated in from the kitchen. Since I didn't enjoy being Tessa and Bennet's third wheel, I asked, "Are you free now? We can go to the café downstairs."

"What about them?" he asked, jerking his chin toward the other room.

"Oh, they're just flirting." I grabbed my jacket. "If we leave them alone, maybe they'll finally get a room somewhere. Tess, Bennet, going for coffee!"

"Don't rush back," Tessa called.

"Are you sure she isn't the boss around here?" Dan asked.

"Don't give her any ideas. Come on, we'll take the back stairs."

I led Dan to the rear entrance, and he followed me down the stairs. "Is this how you sneak around?" he asked.

"I don't sneak." The stairway let out into the alleyway between buildings. "But, these stairs are pretty convenient."

Once we were inside the coffee shop, the barista yelled out a greeting and started working on my drink. While that happened, Dan ordered a plain black coffee.

"You come here a lot?" Dan asked.

"You could say caffeine flows through my veins." We collected our drinks and claimed the sole booth in the shop. It was in the back, next to the kitchen, and was as close to private as we could get.

"So." I set my latte on the table, and folded my hands together. "I guess we can start with the million things you want to ask me."

Dan watched me for a moment. "You see spirits, is that right?"

"Technically, I'm a seer. I interact with ghosts." I paused, waiting for a follow-up question. When Dan remained patiently waiting, I continued, "My family have been seers for generations."

"Then you're an expert."

"I know a few things."

"What's the difference between a ghost and a demon?"

"That depends on who you ask. Some claim there are only ghosts, and some are meaner than others," I replied. "Others claim that demons are genuine evil spirits."

"Huh." Dan sampled his coffee, then asked, "Which do you believe?"

I tapped the table with my index finger, remembering the series of incidents that led up to me leaving town eleven years ago. "I am honestly not sure."

"It's not like regular people can't get up to evil all on their own," Dan said, and I nodded. "Any idea who this Nathaniel spirit is supposed to be?"

"We—Tessa, Bennet, and I—are still researching that."

"You let a lot of people in on your secret?"

"As of right now you are the third living person in town who's in the club."

"Living, huh?" Dan leaned back against the booth and stretched his arm across the top, while his gaze focused on the poster to our left; it was all about where coffee beans came from. My focus never left Dan. He was being remarkably calm about having the supernatural world thrown at him.

Maybe Tessa was right, and I'd misjudged him.

"How did you find Abigail Stevens?"

I blinked myself back to reality. "A ghost told me where to find her."

"Do you get a lot of help from ghosts on your cases?"

"Not usually. Dead people have better things to do than harass the living. Well, usually they do."

"Are there any ghosts here now?"

I glanced around. "Nope. Why? Waiting for a message from beyond?"

Dan's phone buzzed. "Speaking of Casper." He checked it, and said, "Duty calls. Want to come with me? Scene's still fresh."

"You want to bring me to an active crime scene?"

"Why not? Maybe we can get a ghostly intervention. Besides, my coffee's still hot. Date's still on."

"This is not a date. Who's driving?"

***

Dan drove. He didn't have a police cruiser, or one of those boring undercover vehicles. Instead, we piled into a brand new and very shiny black sport utility vehicle.

"Is this your real car?" I asked.

"No, it's my fake car," he replied. "What kind of a question is that?"

"A legitimate one. Is it legal for you to bring your own car to a crime scene?"

"Speaking of legal, how many weapons do you have on you right now?"

I went still. "What makes you think I have any weapons?"

"Back at the Allwoods' you had a self-defense baton hidden in your pant leg, and razorblades sewn into your waistband," he replied. "Being a PI rougher work than you expected?"

"Sometimes. Most of the time all I do is some online research, maybe hit up the library, and hand over what I find to the client. Occasionally I have to follow people, and I never know where I'll end up."

"It's good to be prepared. Maybe you should hire a bodyguard."

"I don't need a bodyguard."

Dan's gaze slid toward me, then he refocused on the road. "Says the girl with razorblades sewn into her jeans. Where'd you get the idea for that, anyway?"

The memory of being tied up and left in a dark, damp basement took hold of me. I clenched my fists and turned my face toward the window, and concentrated on the sound of the engine, the rhythm of the tires against the road. After a few deep breaths, I said, "I don't want to talk about that right now."

"Fair enough. We're headed to an unattended death."

I blinked, simultaneously shocked and relieved that Dan was willing to let his prior line of questioning go. "Is that why you're bringing me? To see if there's a ghost nearby who can crack your case?"

"Maybe. Or maybe I want to see the legendary Eliza Moore in action." I started to call him a moron, but he pulled over and parked. "We're here."

Here turned out to be fifty-four Suffolk Street, which was a two story brick home with a well-kept lawn on a quiet street. As unattended deaths went, this one had probably been peaceful. I followed Dan up the front walk, but a uniformed officer barred me from entering the house.

"She's with me," Dan said. "Consultant."

The officer looked me up and down as if he didn't believe Dan, but he held up the police tape for us. We ducked under the tape and entered the home, and followed the sound of voices into the kitchen.

Our victim was seated at the kitchen table, their head resting in a puddle of vomit. As my coffee turned to lava in my stomach, I realized that the pervading scent in the kitchen wasn't the decedent's last meal. It was something sweet, and heavy.

"Hello, everyone. What have we got?" Dan asked.

"According to the call sheet, our victim was last seen four days ago," another officer replied. His badge told me he was called Meyers. "When his neighbors got worried they called in a well-being check, and here we are."

"Here we are, indeed." Dan looked around the modest kitchen. "He own the place?"

"This house is owned by a corporation. We're looking into it now."

"But he is the owner," Dan said. "Isn't he?"

"We're not sure," Officer Meyers replied. "He doesn't have any identification, and we can't find anything in the house with a name on it."

"That's weird," I said. "No mail, prescription bottles, old letters?"

"None of that," he replied. "At least, not on the first floor. The team's searching upstairs now."

I sidled over to the kitchen trash can and opened the lid. It was so clean it looked like it had just been purchased.

"We did check the trash," the officer examining the body said.

"Sorry," I said. "Force of habit."

She extended a gloved hand toward me, then thought better of it. "I'm Jill, forensics."

"Eliza," I said. "Detective Lyons dragged me along."

Jill narrowed her eyes toward Dan. "Did he."

"You're telling me we have a possible John Doe, dead in a house he may or may not own?" Dan asked, ignoring Jill.

Officer Meyers nodded. "Yes, sir. That's where we are."

"Interesting." Dan leaned closer to the body. "He hasn't been dead four days. What's up with his hands?" I looked closer, and saw that the victim's fingers were covered with angry red bumps.

"Dermatitis," I answered, startling Dan and the other officers. "It happens when you touch something toxic, like poison ivy."

Dan nodded. "Do we think dermatitis killed him?"

"That's not likely," I said. "It's basically just an itchy rash."

Jill nodded. "We'll have to do an autopsy to determine if his death was from natural causes."

"He's pretty well-dressed for a guy hanging out in his kitchen," Dan said. I glanced at the body; he was wearing the sort of well-tailored yet bland clothing the very rich favored. His button-down shirt was a heavy cotton weave, his pants were impeccably pressed, his shoes were buttery soft loafers, and his ensemble was topped off with an actual satin smoking jacket.

"His clothes don't match this house," I said.

"No, they do not," Dan agreed.

I moved around the table to get a better look at the victim, and caught another whiff of the same sweet odor. I wondered if the cloying scent that hung over the room was an expensive cologne, but it was too familiar to me for it to be something store bought. This was a natural scent.

"Was the house closed up when you found him?" I asked, still trying to pinpoint the source of that scent. "No open windows, no fans running..." I followed my nose to the adjacent laundry room, and found a potted plant sitting on the dryer. Its glossy strap-like leaves and five-petaled pink flowers were a dead giveaway: oleander. Even so, I took a deep breath and confirmed it was the scent I'd recognized.

"Here's your cause of death," I called.

Dan entered the laundry room. "A plant killed this guy?"

"Not just a plant. Oleander," I said. "It's extremely toxic, causes contact dermatitis, cardiac problems, seizures, and death." I indicated the scissors lying next to the planter, and the dried up leaves scattered on top of the dryer and floor. "Looks like someone was pruning it recently."

"I wonder who." Dan took my elbow and walked me back into the kitchen. After he asked the officers to take fingerprints in the laundry room, he opened the kitchen's sliding door and we went out on the patio.

"How sure are you about the oleander?"

"That it's oleander or that it's poisonous?"

"Both."

"One hundred percent," I replied. "My grandmother, she was an expert on poisonous plants."

Dan's forehead creased. "Please tell me she doesn't live in this neighborhood or have a grudge against our victim."

"She's dead. Not by poison," I added.

"My condolences. Do you think the oleander killed him?"

I shrugged. "It's possible. He looks like he was poisoned, what with the vomiting and the rash on his hands."

"All right. Wait here."

I overlooked that he was ordering me around, since it was his crime scene. I leaned on the patio table, and wished I hadn't left my latte in the car. It was probably cold by now, anyway.

Dan returned, and said, "Forensics will take it from here. Let's hit the road."

"That's it?" We walked through the yard rather than through the house. I wondered why that was. "Being a detective is a lot less work than I thought it was."

"What can I say, I brought a brilliant PI along to do my work for me." He grinned, then gestured toward the yard. "See anything you recognize?"

"You mean anything poisonous? No. And before you ask, there aren't any ghosts nearby, either."

"Our victim isn't hanging around?"

"Not at the moment." I took a second look around the yard. It was a square of neatly trimmed lawn, without any shrubs or flowers in sight. "You know, it is weird that he had an oleander in his house."

"Really? How so?"

"He has no other landscaping, just grass, yet inside he has a single very exotic, very well-cared for oleander." I shook my head. "People who are into plants are like addicts. They can never have just one, and they're always buying more. I find it hard to believe an oleander was his starter houseplant."

"I didn't see any plants at your place."

"Mine are in my bedroom, and my grandmother's solarium. I go out there a couple times a week."

We got to the SUV, and Dan opened the door for me. "Did Carrington ask you to meet him at the greenhouse because of all your plant knowledge?"

"Funnily enough, the only thing I know about corpse flowers is that they stink like corpses."

"I can't believe that's their real name."

"I know, right?" I watched the neighborhood go by. "Bennet told me that those plants—the corpse flowers—take a notoriously long time to bloom, then all of a sudden all three of his were all about to bloom at once. Bennet though it might mean something sinister was about to happen, so he called me. When I got to the greenhouse the plants had been arranged in such a way they resembled a summoning ritual."

"Really." Dan leaned over and popped open the glove box. "There's a notebook and some pens in there. Can you draw how everything was set up?"

"Sure." I found what I needed and set about sketching how the flower pots had been set up.

"Who set up the plants?"

"Nick Allwood. He claimed Nathaniel made him do it."

"I'm starting to wonder if Nick's as innocent as he claims." Dan steered into a drive through and ordered two black coffees at the speaker.

"What are you doing?"

"I figure you'll keep hanging out with me as long as I keep buying you coffee." He smiled sheepishly, and added, "I'll buy you lunch, too, if you want."

"So you're bribing me with caffeine and food?"

"Sure am." He paid at the window and accepted our coffees. After he handed me a cup, he asked, "Is it working?"

"I guess. I hadn't planned on getting kidnapped by law enforcement today."

"Oh? How exactly would you plan for it?"

"I would have worn different shoes, for one."

"All right, all right. I get it." Dan made a few more turns, and soon we were on the street that led to my building.

"Listen, I'm not trying to be a creep," he said. "I appreciate everything you've told me. I know that can't have been easy."

"I appreciate you taking me seriously. Most people either assume I'm nuts, or looking for attention."

"Hard to deny what I saw with my own eyes." He parked in the lot adjacent to my building. "Can you handle the lovebirds? I can walk you up, if you'd like."

"Love—Oh, you mean Tessa and Bennet? They're harmless. Thanks for the coffee." I put my hand on the door handle, and paused. "I don't think you're a creep, and despite what I said at the time I am so glad you followed me to the Allwoods' house. Thank you for that."

"You better go. If you keep saying such nice things to me I'll get ideas. Oh, hang on." Dan grabbed his phone and keyed something in. A moment later my phone chirped.

"Now you have my personal cell," he said. "If you go after any other suspected demons or whatever, call me. I'll back you up."

"I told you, I don't need a bodyguard."

"But sometimes you need help. You did the other day, and you did when whatever happened that made you hide weapons and razors all over yourself. All I'm saying is that if you think you might need help again, call."

"You're not going to follow me around, waiting for me to slip up?"

"I am not, but I am going to do another background check on Allwood. Something's not right."

"Agreed. Hey, if you need help, call me. I can back you up, too."

He laughed. "Will do. See you around, Eli."

CHAPTER 7

THIS ALL SOUNDS A LITTLE HOKEY

The day after Dan brought me to the unattended death scene, I got an email from him stating that the courts decided Nick Allwood wasn't a criminal, and the state's case against him had been dropped. The official explanation was that Jada had suffered some sort of trauma when she was younger, but she'd hidden it from those around her, including Nick. When they'd recently relocated, Jada had had some kind of relapse, which accounted for what had happened in the town house. Nick came out looking like a brother who was trying desperately to care for his mentally challenged sister.

As alibis and explanations went, it was pretty lame. It was also the fastest court decision in history, which made me wonder if the officials were hiding something. But the people who needed to believe it signed off on that version of events, and no one was asking me any questions, and that was what mattered.

I'd gone to visit Jada in the hospital yesterday afternoon, for all the good it did either of us. Mentally, she was an eight-year-old girl, and acted as if no time had passed since that day with the fairy mirror. Her doctors were confident they could help her regain her memory of the last twenty years. I wasn't sure that was a good idea, but I kept my opinions to myself. Now that they'd conveniently labeled the whole situation as a memory issue, I was definitely not offering advice.

I moved the email to a folder labeled "Detective Lyons", relabeled the folder "Dan", then I shut my laptop and set about watering the plants; Gran would have been proud. My potted belladonna was by far my favorite, even though she required the most upkeep. For now, she was happy underneath her grow light, and I'd picked up a bunch of clearance Easter lilies at the grocery store to keep her company. So far, everyone was getting along well.

Watering complete, I set down the pitcher and surveyed my apartment. I still didn't have as many plants as I wanted, though I hadn't lived here for very long. I understood it would take time to create an indoor jungle like Gran's solarium, especially since the plants I wanted weren't offered in the average nursery. That meant I needed to source seeds either in the wild or from sketchy mail order companies, two actions that took time and patience.

The easiest and fastest method would be to take some specimens from Gran's solarium and bring them here. I was certain she wouldn't mind, although the cats—a trio of terror everyone referred to as the Feline Federation—would be irritated if something got moved around. Since the cats were ghosts, I wasn't too concerned about them staying mad. What did concern me was my reluctance to deal with Gran's house.

It's not like I was letting the place rot. I went there several times a week to care for the plants, play with the cats, and check the mail and phone messages; tons of people still reached out to Gran, testament to her excellent reputation as a seer, a listener, and a friend. What I was letting rot was the Moore's reputation as seers.

I didn't want to take Gran's place. I couldn't, since no matter how much knowledge and experience I accumulated, I would never be her. But, I could make myself a bit more visible in the supernatural community, and maybe that would be enough to keep everything Gran had built from crumbling to dust.

How to begin, how to begin. Being visible was easier said than done; it's one thing to want to be a member of a community, and another to go out and do the work. Since one of Gran's favorite lessons was about being efficient, I decided to go to the city administrator's office and search the archives for the name Nathaniel. It was a very common name, but it could have been the surname of a once-prominent family. I might run across building plans for a Nathaniel Hall, or an article about the ribbon cutting ceremony at a Nathaniel Park. Even if I didn't find any significant mentions of the name, I might uncover something else of importance. Another of Gran's lessons was that all research went toward the greater good.

After I'd settled on the bare bones of the day's plan, I showered and picked out a navy blue dress decorated with tiny daisies. It was a little much for a municipal office, but I wasn't going out not as Eli Moore, PI. Instead, I would be stepping out as Eliza Moore, scion of the Moore seers, and that was certainly a dress-worthy cause.

I paired the dress with my usual leather jacket and boots. Don't want to stray too far from my established image. As I gave my apartment a final once-over before heading out, my office phone rang.

"Nine Lives Investigations," I greeted.

"Hello, may I speak to Miss Moore?"

I'd know that posh accent anywhere. "Hello, Nick. It's me. What can I do for you?"

"Oh. Hello, Miss Moore. Would you mind terribly if I stopped by your office?"

"Do you have a case for me?"

"I do not." He paused, and I heard him clear his throat. "I would like to talk to you about Jada. I suspect you're one of the few who truly understands the situation."

I understood why he wouldn't want to have that conversation over the phone. "Okay. I'm here now, so just swing on by."

We ended the call, then I took off my jacket and draped it over the back of my chair. I was mildly disappointed that my plans had been changed, mostly because I'd gotten dressed up for nothing. Then again, Gran used to counsel people in her home, so maybe me speaking with Nick was the best way to honor her.

"You look like a lady, for once."

Startled, I looked up and saw Prudence, the ghost who'd led me to Abigail Stevens, standing in front of my desk. "Thanks. You look the same as ever." Prudence turned her nose up and scowled at my computer. For a ghost who refused to move on, she absolutely hated modern life and all the technology that came with it.

"Do you know what happened recently at the college," I began, then I told Prudence all about the corpse flowers, exorcism of Jada, and the possible involvement of a Nathaniel.

"Praise God you were able to save that poor girl," Prudence said when I'd finished. "As for your responsible spirits, I've encountered none called Nathaniel. Are you certain that's the proper name?"

"I'm not," I admitted. "Is there any way you could poke around for me? I don't want this spirit finding his way toward any other girls."

Prudence nodded sharply. "I shall do what I can," she said before dissipating. Prudence and I didn't always see eye to eye, what with me scandalously living alone and unmarried, but we did agree that children were to be protected at all costs. I was confident she would help me in any way she could.

There was a knock at my office door. That must be Nick.

"Hello," I said when I opened the door. "You got here fast."

"I was in the neighborhood."

I stepped aside and gestured to my office. "Well, come on in."

"Thank you. And thank you for agreeing to see me," he said. Nicholas wasn't his usual refined self. His blond hair was tousled, and he was wearing jeans and a wrinkled pullover. He still wore his wire rimmed glasses, so that was something.

"Of course." I shut the door behind him and indicated the couch in the waiting area. "Have a seat. Would you like some tea?"

"Please."

I retreated to the kitchen. The electric kettle quickly heated the water, then I brought two steaming mugs of English breakfast tea out to the waiting area.

"I heard that the state dropped its case against you," I handed him a mug, and sat beside him on the couch. "Congratulations on being a free man."

"But that's just it," he began. "I'm not free. I'm still responsible for my sister, and now that she's back to being just her I've no idea what to do with her."

I imagined most men wouldn't know what to do with a physically adult, yet mentally childish sibling. "Have the doctors given you an update on Jada?"

"Only to regale me with tales of my sister's wonderful physical health," he replied. "I'm told it's a miracle that she's in such good shape. Apparently individuals with these sorts of psychiatric disorders are usually quite frail." He laughed noiselessly into his tea. "If they only knew that she was so healthy because I'd forced her to eat, and to bathe, and to rest when her body needed it. I've gone so far as to force vitamins down her throat. I never once gave up hope that my sister would be returned to me. And she was, thanks to you."

"I didn't have much of a choice," I said. "It was either free Jada, or let Bennet, Dan, and possible you and me die. Luckily we all got out of there."

Nicholas set his mug on the coffee table. "Luck had nothing to do with it. You, Miss Moore, are our savior."

I felt my face warm from my cheeks down to my cleavage. "I'm no savior. I only wanted to help."

"Help us you did." Nick moved closer to me. "I truly don't know how I'll ever thank you."

As his blue eyes gazed into mine, I thought up a few ways he could thank me. Here was an intelligent, caring, and attractive man who'd seen the supernatural side of things and hadn't run off screaming. Maybe the old adage about seers staying with their own kind was wrong, and I could find happiness with a mortal. Maybe all of my relationships didn't have to end in failure, like my father's had.

Maybe I wasn't doomed to live alone.

Nick put his hand on my knee. I could feel the heat of him through my thin dress.

"You don't need to thank me." My stomach was in knots. It had been years since I let someone get so close to me, and I had half a mind to run. "I only did what anyone would do."

"That's where you're wrong, Miss Moore. Very, very few would have done what you did."

"My friends call me Eliza, or Eli."

"Eliza," he said, rolling my name around his mouth. "Such a beautiful name." Nick slid his hand underneath my hair and stroked the back of my neck. He paused, and when I didn't pull away he leaned in and kissed me.

Fireworks.

"Nick," I gasped when we parted. I was against parting, but this guy had recently tied me up—twice—and chloroformed me. The latter had left me with a headache for days. "What are we doing?"

"Forgive me," he murmured, as his thumb glided across my cheekbone. "Since we met at the greenhouse, you're all I can think about."

"What were you thinking about when you put a sack over my head?"

"I had no choice," he said. "The entity inside my sister insisted, and if I hadn't done as she'd asked she would have harmed Jada." His blue eyes gazed into mine, and he said, "It had harmed Jada in the past."

"Really?" Jada's body had seemed in good health to me, but not all abuse leaves scars. "That must have been awful."

"It was." Nick tucked a lock of my hair behind my ear. "Your hair is the same rich brown as your eyes. Fascinating."

"It's a family trait," I said, because who doesn't want to talk about hereditary eye color while wrapped in a passionate embrace? "My grandfather, he was Indian."

"Was he?" Nick asked, then he kissed me again.

Again, fireworks.

This time, I kissed him back.

I'd never felt such an instant connection with someone, almost as if electricity coursed throughout our bodies. Nick must have felt it too, and he wrapped his arms around me and pulled me against his chest. One of his hands glided down my back to my hip, then he pulled my leg up onto his lap. In another moment I'd be on my back beneath him.

We were moving incredible fast but I didn't want him to stop. I wanted him to take me, right there on the waiting room couch.

Nick's hand moved underneath my skirt.

I still didn't stop him.

His hand moved higher, above my knee, then it stroked down to my calf.

A shock jolted us apart.

"What was that?" he demanded. We moved apart as fast as we'd come together.

"A warning." I felt the side of my leg; Nick's touch had activated one of my protection tattoos. My skin still buzzed from the warning. "I think you should go."

"Eliza, I'd like to talk about this."

"We will, but later."

He frowned, then he got up and left without another word. I grabbed my phone and sent a text to Dan.

Me: Working?
Dan: Yeah. Off in an hour. Why?
Me: Want to meet tonight? Need to talk about a thing.
Dan: You got it.

***

I met Dan at the diner across the street from my building a few hours after Nick left my place. During those hours I'd gone for a run, showered, and put on jeans and a tee shirt. I might never wear a dress again.

The diner was one of those refurbished train cars, complete with polished chrome walls and a neon sign over the door. The menu was pretty standard, which meant I didn't eat there often. I'm not a food snob, but working for myself meant I didn't have health insurance. That meant no greasy fries for me. It did not mean I didn't stare longingly at the fries on other people's plates.

Dan arrived before me. I found him at a booth near the front, staring at the tableside juke box. He'd just ended his shift, and had mentioned he was starving. I wondered if he was wearing a gun. After what had happened with Nick, I hoped he was.

"Hey," I said as I slid into the booth.

"I ordered for you," he said by way of greeting. I started to say that I was perfectly capable of ordering for myself, when the waitress plunked down a white porcelain mug and filled it with coffee.

"Thanks," I said. After leaving us with a couple menus, the waitress left us alone.

"I wasn't sure if you drank coffee this late," Dan said. "I almost got you a milkshake."

"That would have been fine, as long as it was chocolate." I stirred creamer into my mug. "Thanks for meeting me."

"You can thank me by telling me what's up."

"What makes you think anything's up?"

He gave me a look. "Eli, something's always up with you."

I bit my lip. I wanted to argue with him, but he was right. I needed help, and Dan was the only person I could go to.

"Something's going on with Nick Allwood," I began.

"Going on how? Is he," Dan leaned across the table and whispered, "possessed?"

"No. Maybe. I don't think so." I leaned back in the booth and gently batted the salt shaker between my hands. "He came to my office earlier today to talk about Jada."

Dan shook his head. "That poor kid. She show any improvement?"

"She's a perfectly healthy and happy eight year old girl, living in a twenty-eight year old body," I replied. "It's like her entire awareness shut down the moment she was possessed. She knows nothing about being an adult, or even a teenager."

Dan picked up the laminated menu and scanned the appetizers. "What happened after he told you the update about Jada?"

"He touched one of my tattoos, and I got a warning shock."

Dan set down the menu. "You have tattoos? And they warn you about... What do they warn you about?"

I unbuckled the watch from my left hand. Instead of a traditional band, the timepiece was on a long strip of leather that would around my wrist several times. Dan watched me as I removed the band and revealed the tattoo beneath.

"I have several tattoos. This is my seer's mark."

I laid my arm on the table palm up. On the inner skin of my wrist was a symbol tattooed in cobalt blue ink. It was all circles and lines; anyone who wasn't a seer would assume it was abstract art.

Dan reached toward my wrist, halting himself before he made contact with my skin. "May I?" he asked, his hand hovering above me.

"Go ahead."

Permission granted, he traced the lines of my tattoo. Shivers coursed down my spine as I willed myself to stay still. "Are you getting anything from me?"

"No warnings," I replied, and that was the truth.

"So this tattoo is what makes you a seer?"

"You're either born a seer or you're not. These marks are meant to help protect us. We tend to deal with otherworldly forces that can often appear innocent."

"Is this symbol some kind of warning sigil?"

"Not the symbol itself. The designs are unique to each seer."

Dan cradled my wrist in his hands and peered at my tattoo. "It's the ink, then?"

"Yeah," I said, unable to keep the surprise from my voice. "How'd you know that?"

"I figure stuff out for a living." He flashed me a quick smile, then resumed scrutinizing my wrist. "What's it made of? The ink, that is."

"I don't know," I replied. "The tattooist makes each ink so it's unique to the bearer."

"Do you get to pick out the design?"

"The marksman—that's what we call the person who does the tattoos—meditates in solitude, and comes up with the tattoo's design and formula for the ink. When he comes out of his trance, the work begins."

"You'll forgive me for saying so, but this all sounds a little hokey," Dan said as he released my wrist. "This marksman seems like a stoner trying to give his subjects a contact high."

"The current marksman is my father."

Dan's eyes went wide. "Okay. Well. I'm sure he's a perfectly respectable guy."

I sipped some coffee. "Nice save."

"Let's say you have a tattoo that can ring a magical warning bell. How could it have done so through that thick leather wristband?"

"It wasn't this tattoo," I replied. "Dad hooked me up with a bunch of protection symbols. Nick touched the tattoo on my lower leg."

"Same question. How did all this magic work through jeans?"

"I was wearing a dress at the time."

Dan set down his mug with a bang. "You wore a dress for him?"

"I was already wearing a dress, then he came over!"

"You've never worn a dress for me."

"I don't wear anything for you!" Dan laughed; after a moment, I joined him. "You know what I mean."

"Wardrobe choices aside, what does this warning mean?" Dan asked. "You said he's not possessed."

"I don't know exactly, but something's not right. He's hiding something, and it might be something big."

"What can I do to help?"

"I think we need to talk to Bennet."

***

After a quick call to ensure that Bennet was home and wouldn't mind visitors, Dan and I drove across town to his house. Instead of the black SUV from yesterday, Dan was driving a white sedan.

"Is this your cop car?" I teased. "Do you transport perps in the back?"

Dan's gaze slid toward me. "Why? Want me to handcuff you?"

"Go ahead. Cuffs won't hold me for long."

"Gonna get a ghost to bring you the key?"

"No. I have a set of lock picks and I know how to use them."

Dan laughed. "Of course you do."

A twenty-minute drive later, and we arrived at Bennet's house. It was a cape style home with those triangle-shaped second floor windows, and it wouldn't have been out of place in the English countryside. The front yard was neat and well-tended, not that I expected anything less from a master horticulturist.

"How long have you known Dr. Carrington?" Dan asked. He parked on the street in front of the cottage, and we exited the vehicle.

"All my life," I replied. "Bennet is an old friend of my grandmother's. I think he's the only shepherd in the area."

"He has sheep?"

"Not that sort of shepherd. In the seer community a shepherd is a point of contact. We tend to be spread pretty far apart."

"Why is that, I wonder," Dan mused. "You're not sure if he's the only shepherd around here?"

"Gran never said how many shepherds are nearby. If you really want to know how many are in the area, we can ask him." I surveyed the full to bursting borders packed with lavender, roses, and rosemary. "Hm."

"Are you judging his gardening skills?"

"Bennet's skills are top notch. I was just noticing that none of the plants are poisonous."

"Isn't that a good thing?"

I shrugged. "Definitely safer for pets and kids."

We reached the front door and Dan knocked. A moment later Bennet opened the door and ushered us inside. We followed him through a few rooms packed with books and jarred, dried herbs, and into the dining room. In true British style Bennet had tea waiting in a porcelain pot, which he poured into three matching teacups. The look on Dan's face as he picked up the dainty cup was priceless.

"Eli, you said you had something to discuss," Bennet said after we'd sampled and approved of our tea.

"Your assistant Mr. Allwood came by my office earlier," I began, and I told Bennet how my tattoo had warned me against Nicholas.

"Interesting," Bennet said. He got up and retrieved a notebook and pencil, and set them before me. "Would you mind drawing your tattoo?"

"Not at all." I did, then I slid the notebook back to Bennet.

"Protection from magical combat," Bennet said after he'd reviewed my drawing. "Your father certainly left you well protected."

"You know Eli's father?" Dan asked.

"Oh, yes. Alexander Moore is something of a legend in our circles."

"Does that mean Eli's also a legend?"

"Eli is sitting right here," I snapped. "And no, I do not have the same name recognition as my father and grandmother did. I'm more of a low-key, try to avoid trouble kind of girl." I flopped back in my chair. "For all the good that's doing me."

"You're doing quite well, I'd say," Bennet said. "Well enough to have expunged the entity calling itself Nathaniel, and detected that something else is off about Nicholas."

"About that guy," Dan began. "How well do you know him?"

"I don't really know him at all," Bennet replied. "The school advertised for an assistant horticulturist, he sent in his resume, and was hired. I had nothing to do with it. I didn't even meet him until his first day on the job."

"Nick made it seem like you and he were friends," I said. "The sort of friends who would share occult knowledge."

Bennet shook his head. "That is simply not the case."

"Nick also said that you told him you'd found some information about Nathaniel," I pressed. "That you thought he was an Indonesian demon."

"Nicholas told me that he'd found evidence of Nathaniel being of Indonesian origin," Bennet said. "That was the information he used to lure me to his home."

The three of us looked at each other, then Dan whipped out his phone and walked away from the table. After a short conversation, he said, "I've requested all of the information we have on Allwood. If he's dirty, there'll be a trail."

"Then what?" I asked.

"We follow it, and find out what's really going on."

CHAPTER 8

A FLASH OF FORESIGHT

A FEW HOURS LATER, Dan brought me home from Bennet's, and the ride was devoid of his tired jokes and drive through coffee. Actually, his jokes weren't that bad, and I appreciated the drinks. He wasn't bad company, either, but now that Gran was gone, I wasn't used to being frank with anyone about my abilities. Dan seemed trustworthy enough, but I'd been betrayed before. Most recently, I'd been betrayed by the first guy I'd kissed in longer than I cared to remember. Just a matter of time before it happens again.

"You good?" Dan asked when he pulled up in front of my building.

"What's that supposed to mean?" I snapped.

"Just checking in."

I felt like banging my head against the passenger window. "Sorry. I feel like every one of my nerves has been gone over with sandpaper."

"Want to talk about it?" When I remained silent, he continued. "You never told me how Allwood got close enough to touch your tattoo."

"We were sitting on the couch in my waiting room. And he kissed me."

"Did he hurt you?" Dan demanded. "Or try to hurt you?"

"He didn't. The warning hurt, but it's supposed to."

"Oh." Dan mulled that over for a moment. "What does it feel like?"

"Ever touch an electric fence? Like that."

"That certainly gets some attention." I watched Dan's reflection in the window. He was pensive, studying my profile. "Do you have an easily accessible protection mark?"

I faced him. "Why?"

"Just wondering if you'll get a warning about me."

I thought that was nonsense. Could I even get a warning about a mortal? I shrugged my right arm out of my jacket and presented my arm to Dan. The protection tattoo was a small magenta symbol below my elbow.

"Pretty," Dan said. "Your father's a great artist. May I?"

"Yeah. Go ahead."

Dan grasped my arm and stroked his thumb across my tattoo. Holy hell, every time Dan touched me, he set off every nerve ending I had. "Get anything?"

"If there was a warning, you'd feel it too," I replied, remembering how the shock had knocked Nick away from me.

"Looks like I'm safe." Dan grinned at me. He really was handsome, and kind, and for a brief moment I wondered what would happen if I let my guard down. Then the back of my neck tingled, and my entire body stiffened.

Dan, on the floor.

Is he okay?

Me holding him, desperate to save him.

I blinked myself back to reality. I'd gotten a flash of foresight.

"What's wrong?" Dan demanded.

"Nothing. I..." I debated not telling him what I'd seen, but valued the trust we'd built between us. "Do you know what foresight is?"

Dan cocked his head to the side. "As in, seeing the future?"

"No. Well, yes, but it's not that simple." I slid my arm back into my jacket. "Foresight is random, and fickle, and whenever it comes you get no context for the images. What you see could happen tomorrow, or in twenty years."

"What did you see just now?" When I didn't answer, he asked, "Was it about me?"

"Yeah. You were... I think you we're hurt." I closed my eyes, and replayed the images in my head. "You were on a floor."

"Was I dead?"

"No. You were breathing."

"That's something." I opened my eyes. Dan was watching me, his face guarded. "Do you want to tell me anything else?"

"I want to think about it first. This is the problem with foresight. I get a bunch of images, and they don't make sense." I dropped my gaze to my hands in my lap. "If I misinterpret an image, and tell you something that's not right..."

"Don't worry about it," he said. "I've lived this long without knowing my future. I can go a little longer."

"You really aren't half bad, you know that?"

I expected a joke. Instead he squeezed my forearm. "Get some rest, kid. You look beat."

"You too, Dan."

I got out of the sedan, and headed inside my building.

Despite what Dan said about me looking beat, I was so wired I could barely contemplate sleep. My vision about Dan had freaked me out, and I needed to find a way to relax. Since there wasn't anything I could do about the vision, I decided to get some work done.

I liked being in my office outside business hours. It was quiet, and if I kept the lights off the street lights slanted through the blinds and made the room look like a noir film. That may or may not have been a factor when I decided to move into this place. The balcony had been a nice perk, too.

I sat at my desk and turned on my computer. While it powered up I jotted down what I knew about the Allwoods. One thing I wanted to figure out was where Nick and Jada had been between the afternoon I'd spent with the fairy mirror back in third grade, and when Nick landed his position as assistant horticulturist. Only twenty years of history to figure out, no big.

I sketched out the beginning of a timeline. The afterschool group Jada and I had belonged to was in a city a few towns over from the one I currently lived in; my mother had specifically moved us there because she hadn't wanted to be too close to my grandmother. Or my father, for that matter, not that he was ever home. Nick's current address was in town, and he'd mentioned that he and Jada had inherited the place from an aunt. That made me wonder how long the Allwoods had been in the area.

I sent Bennet an email asking for a copy of Nick's resume; I would have texted him, but he tended to lose his phone. Email sent, I pulled up the property records for Nick's home. The current house had been built in the middle of the eighteenth century by a family called Allwood.

These earlier Allwoods had already owned the land the house was built on. I kept poking, and found an odd bit of folklore tied to that plot of land. Apparently an old witch had lived on the edge of the forest, and in her garden grew nothing but poisonous plants. If you weren't careful, she'd feed your children a pie made from poisoned apples.

I flopped back in my chair, reading and re-reading the snippet. Whoever this ancestor of the Allwoods was, she'd been a witch. The poison garden is what clinched it; most see a plant as either toxic or safe, but the natural world doesn't work in absolutes. Seers and witches worked with the whole plant, and used the toxicity to achieve their goals, be they clairvoyance, healing, or a simple meditative trance. Instead of toxicity rendering a plant useless, we saw poisons as tools to help us understand the world around us.

In fact, my gran lived an almost identical life to the witch's described in the folk tale; she was an old lady living on the edge of the woods, and everything in her garden could kill you. Gran's property backed up to the woods and she kept her plants in an indoor solarium, and as far as I knew she'd never offed anyone with a pie, but the similarities were startling.

Nick and Jada were descended from witches. So why weren't they witches themselves?

I put that information aside for the moment; I wouldn't get any further until I got more information about Nick, and that wouldn't happen until Bennet sent over the resume. Giving my brain a break from the Allwood drama, I looked over the clients Tessa had booked for me. Chasing Nick's history was interesting and necessary, but I needed paying clients in order to pay the bills. As I shuffled through the intake sheets I noted that they were all typical cases; background checks, insurance surveillance, and a desperate plea from a woman who insisted her husband was cheating on her, but one stood out to me.

The prospective client wanted me to surveil a neighbor, to find evidence to bring to the town and get them fined for public health violations. Apparently this neighbor, who owned Stone Creek Orchard, had a surplus of rotting fruit which the client wanted cleaned up. I had no idea what the fresh to rotted fruit ratio was at the average orchard, but Tessa added the following statement: The neighbor claimed the orchard's owner needed to let the fruit rot so he could strain out the seeds.

I searched for the orchard's website, and confirmed it was an apple orchard. Little known fact, apple seeds contain cyanide. Since most people don't eat the seeds it's not really an issue; that, and you'd have to eat hundreds or thousands of apple seeds to approach toxicity. If I was going to kill someone with fruit I'd use cherry pits, which would give you the same effect a whole lot faster. Then again, if I was going to kill someone I would find a more efficient method than murder by fruit.

I clicked around the orchard's website, and found a page with the farm's history. It was currently owned by Jacob Allwood, and had been in his family for generations. Grandma Allwood was well known for her delicious apple pies.

Nick Allwood's house was built on land where an old lady used to feed children poisoned apple pies.

On a hunch, I searched Jacob Allwood. He owned the Allwood Compound, which was the largest property in town, residential or otherwise. The property records didn't say as much, but I knew that those Allwoods were a witch clan.

"What in the hell is happening?" I muttered, as I stared at my screen.

This can't be for real. Not only were clues and witches stacking up, why was everything in my life suddenly connected to poisonous or otherwise unusual plants? Ever since the incident at the retirement home—the belladonna caper, as Bennet called it—everywhere I turned a poison suddenly appeared, whether it was the aforementioned belladonna, or foxglove, and now apple seeds.

If I didn't know better, I'd say someone knew I was a seer and was trying to draw me out.

I held my head in my hands, wondering why any of this was happening. Gran hadn't hidden her abilities, but she hadn't advertised them, either. Most had thought she was a nice lady who spent a lot of time in her garden, not the most powerful seer on the east coast tending her solarium filled with toxic and hallucinogenic plants. Ever since my father left the area to pursue his own calling, she had been the only seer in the region, except for me.

Although, that hadn't always been the case. I remembered dozens of seers coming to visit Gran on a regular basis when I was younger. Bennet came by regularly, too, but I was almost certain he had no abilities of his own. If he was what I suspected, an active shepherd, he would have information on all the seer clans in the region.

I sent him a second email asking about the Allwoods, then I shut my laptop and set the alarm on my phone for six. If the people at Stone Creek Orchard were hoarding apple seeds, I wanted to know why.

Chapter 9

Apples and Bones

Stone Creek Orchard was just beyond the edge of town, near my grandmother's house. That wasn't odd, in and of itself. Witches and seers had always existed near one another, mostly so each group could keep an eye on the other. The supernatural community was not a trusting lot.

I pulled into the field that served as the orchard's parking lot, exited my car and checked out the scene. The closest structure was a red painted clapboard building that a real estate agent would call rustic, but was in reality was a dilapidated old shack. The produce bins out front were empty, and I didn't see anyone else around, but since it wasn't apple season, that didn't surprise me. What did surprise me was when I approached the building and got a look at the rows of apple trees behind it.

They were all covered in glossy green leaves, their branches heavy with fruit.

"This makes no sense," I muttered. Apple trees shouldn't even be blooming for a few more weeks, yet these trees were ready for harvest.

I grabbed my phone from my back pocket, snapped a picture of the trees, and sent it to Tessa. She texted back in less than a minute.

Tessa: Is this real time?

Eli: Sure is. Ever hear of fruit ripening at the wrong time of year?

Tessa: Old witch trick. Let me ask a few questions and get back to you.

I put my phone away and tried the door on the clapboard building. Locked. Since farms have barns and sheds scattered about the property, I figured that would be where the apples were allegedly rotting. Although, I couldn't smell any rot, and I couldn't see a neighbor in any direction. If the neighbors couldn't see or smell the rotting apples, why would they have complained?

This is not good. I texted my location to Tessa, then I started walking between the trees. I went up and down at least a dozen rows before I found the barn. The doors were wide open, so I stepped inside and looked around. In the center of the main room were four enormous wooden vats.

A likely spot to let apples rot. A catwalk snaked around the vats, presumably so people could monitor whatever was going on inside. I climbed the closest ladder and saw that the vats were full of apples floating in a foamy liquid. Up close, the concoction smelled like cider, and I wondered if a nosy neighbor was trying to shut down a nice witch's homemade cider business.

Something white bobbed in the vat. I grabbed a nearby paddle and poked at the apples until the white object showed itself. It was a human skull.

I dropped the paddle and backed away from the vat, then I called Dan.

"Hey, Eli. Ready for our next coffee date?"

"I'm at Stone Creek Orchard. I've found human remains."

***

"So. This is interesting." Dan gestured toward the barn.

I scowled toward the vats of apples and bones. "That's one word for it."

Dan had beat the uniformed officers and forensics team by five minutes. I'd waited for them by the clapboard building, then led them through the maze of apple trees to the barn of doom. Forensics had secured the barn, and started labeling and photographing everything. Once that was done, they were going to drain the vats and start counting bones.

"Shouldn't there be more people here?" I asked. "You know, investigating?"

"Depends on what the first crew finds," Dan replied. "Right now we have some bones, but a dead body doesn't automatically equal criminal activity. He could have fallen in, had a heart attack, who knows what." Dan glanced around, ensuring we were out of earshot of the rest. "You think it's a he?"

"I have no idea," I replied. "All I know is some mystery neighbor wanted to hire me to find dirt on this orchard."

"Do we know who this neighbor is?"

"Tessa took the information. She's on her way." I approached one of the apple trees. "First corpse flowers start blooming en masse, and now apple trees are going out of season, and we've got a skeleton in the barn. It's like fairy tales gone from bad to worse."

Dan picked one of the apples. "Maybe they used some new kind of fertilizer. Maybe there's nothing weird going on here, just a new breed of trees and a clumsy farmer who tripped and landed in a vat of cider."

"Maybe. Don't eat that."

"Why not?"

"Could be poisonous."

Dan dropped the fruit. I heard a car pull up, and walked to the front of the orchard. "Tessa's here," I called over my shoulder.

Tessa got out of her car holding a file folder against her chest. Even though it was still very early, and we were standing in field, her hair was styled and she was dressed like a golden age Hollywood starlet, complete with heels. "She brought paperwork."

"Paperwork," Dan said. "My favorite."

"First of all, I had no idea that witches might be involved with this case," Tessa said once I got close enough, then she grinned at something over my shoulder. "Hello, Detective Lyons."

"Dan," he said, smiling. Everyone smiled at Tessa, and it had nothing to do with magic. "Call me Dan."

"If you insist." She handed him the folder. "This is everything I know about the potential client. They never came into the office, and instead contacted us through a form on our website. I printed out the initial message, and the one follow-up message they sent." She pointed to something on the sheet. "That's the IP address they used to send both of the messages."

"Good work," Dan said. Tessa preened at the attention.

"This place is owned by the Allwood family," I said. "Have you ever heard of them?"

"Of course I have," Tessa replied. "They used to be the dominant witch clan in this area."

"Used to? What happened to them?" I asked.

Tessa shrugged. "Clans rise, clans fall. It's all very dramatic."

"You say that as if you remember these rises and falls," Dan said.

Tessa smiled coyly. "Imagine that."

"This orchard is owned by a Jacob Allwood," I said, ignoring her flirting. "If he turned up dead, what are the odds witchcraft had something to do with it?"

"If he's the Jacob Allwood I know of, as in the head of the clan, I would say the odds are very good, indeed."

"Have you met him?" I asked.

"Only in passing. The Allwoods and Beauclaires have had their share of run-ins."

"Are you aware that the Nick and Jada from a few weeks ago are named Allwood?" Dan asked.

Tessa's eyes widened. "No, I was not." Tessa bit her lip. "Eliza, do you think this has anything to do with—"

"Probably not," I said. Tessa frowned, but didn't press the matter, which was great. I did not need Dan knowing more about my past than necessary. "Nick and Jada don't seem to be witches, just unlucky mortals. All the witchcraft is happening here."

Speaking of Dan, he was watching both of us like a hawk. "Witch-craft," he said. "As in the craft of witches."

Tessa grinned. "He's handsome and smart."

"Like a Labrador retriever with a badge," I said. "Thanks for bring-ing this by, Tess. I really appreciate it."

"Of course. I put some feelers out earlier, about the off-season fruit. I'll let you know if I hear anything."

"Thanks again. You are a literal lifesaver."

Tessa placed her hand on my cheek. "Don't make me do that again."

With that, Tessa got in her car and left me standing there with a bewildered and curious detective. I took a deep breath, steeling myself for whatever questions he was just waiting to ask.

"Go ahead." When his brows pinched, I added, "I know you have ten thousand questions bubbling away in there. Let's just get it over with."

He regarded me for a moment. "Labrador retriever, really?"

I gave him what I hoped was an apologetic smile. "It was a compli-ment."

"Sure, it was. Are you a witch?"

"No. Witches and seers are different. As far as I know there isn't any overlap between the two."

He nodded. "But Tessa is a witch."

I hesitated, since I didn't like outing people. However, he had figured it out on his own. "She is. And here's a freebie for you to chew on. Tessa is much older than she appears."

"Ooo-kay. Like, sixty years old?"

"More. Way more."

"All right. I am tabling that fact until I can give it the time and brainpower it deserves. Let's see what forensics has for us." He turned toward the clapboard building. "What did you find in there?"

"I didn't go in. It's locked."

"What about your legendary lock picks?"

"Believe it or not, I try to avoid breaking and entering."

"But you do have them." When I nodded, he continued, "Since this is a crime scene, and I'm the lead detective, I find it necessary to enter this building to further our investigation." He approached the door and tried the handle. "Still locked. If only there was someone close by who could help me get inside this building."

"All right. I get it." I crouched in front of the door and withdrew a leather case from my jacket's inner chest pocket. "If you arrest me I'm hiring a lawyer."

Dan watched me open the case of picks. "That looks professional."

"I bought it online. Came with a clear plastic padlock to practice on."

"Fancy."

After a bit of trial and error, I beat the lock and opened the door. Dan pushed it wide open, then he extended his arm across the entrance, barring my way.

"Sorry," he said when I bumped into his arm. "Let me go first."

Dan entered the building. He announced that police were entering; when no one responded he beckoned me inside. We were in a large room that had probably served as the orchard's store. There were glass display cases at one end, next to a lunch counter and an old-fashioned soda fountain. I remembered the story about the poisoned apple pie, and wondered if the health department had ever been called down to investigate the desserts. Everything, from the stools to the syrup pumps, was covered in a thick layer of dust.

"It doesn't look like this place has seen any business this decade," Dan said.

"Or longer. I've never even heard of this orchard, and my gran and I went apple picking every fall."

"You're from around here?"

"As if you don't already know."

"How would I know if you've never told me?"

I faced him. "You've never run a background check on me?"

"I checked to make sure your PI paperwork was up to date, and I ran your criminal history," he replied. "Standard procedure. Other than that, I only know what you tell me."

I closed my eyes, and asked the one question I dreaded more than all others. "None of the police talk about me? No one mentions any weird incidents?"

"The only cop who thinks you show up at all the weird cases is me. The rest of the department likes to give me a hard time about it." He frowned. "This weird incident, does it have anything to do with what Tessa mentioned?"

"Yes." I walked the perimeter of the room, opening doors. The first two led to closets, but the third revealed a set of stairs. "Want to check out the second floor?"

Dan pulled out a flashlight and shone it onto the steps. "Want me to go first?"

"I can handle stairs."

I ascended the stairs, realizing halfway up that it was dark, and I really should have let the guy with the light go first. Oops. When I reached the upper floor, I stepped aside and let Dan and his flashlight illuminate the room.

"Floor seems solid," he said. He put his hand on the small of my back to guide me around the stairwell's opening.

"Sorry," he said. "I should have asked first."

"Why do you always do that?"

"Why do I apologize when I don't ask before I touch you? It's called being respectful."

"You do it constantly. It's annoying."

Dan watched me for a moment. "What happened to you?"

"Nothing."

"Bullshit. You're fiercely independent, which could be construed as a trauma response to being let down by those close to you. You have razors sewn into your clothes, thus leading me to believe you've been tied up at least once before that time at the Allwood house. Add that to the knives, batons, and protection tattoos scattered across your body, and all these clues tell me someone hurt you. Bad." Dan touched the back of my hand. "I know you think I'm just a dumb cop, but I see you, Eli."

For a split second I was in the basement again, could feel the dirt floor, smell the damp rot. "I don't think you're dumb. Or just a cop."

"That's the nicest thing you've ever said to me." He smiled, and the tension lightened between us. "You don't have to tell me what happened. It's none of my business. But, I want you to know that I've got your back. You need me, I'm there."

I swallowed the lump in my throat. "Thanks. That means a lot."

"You're welcome." He swung the beam around the room. "This seems like a standard attic storage room to me."

I felt something graze my forehead. After some embarrassing flailing I realized it was a pull chain for the overhead light. I clicked it on, and we blinked at the sudden brightness. Once my eyes adjusted I saw that the room was almost completely empty, except for a few crates and three barrels tucked into a corner.

"There's not a lot up here." I approached the barrels. "Should we have a look?"

"Why not?"

Dan took the lid off the first barrel. It was filled with apple seeds.

"Well, this is an apple orchard," he said. "Next year's crop, maybe?"

I shook my head. "You propagate fruit trees by grafting, not sowing new seeds, but I've known people to hoard seeds in order to extract cyanide."

Dan went completely still. "There's cyanide in apple seeds?"

"Sure is." I grabbed the lid off the second barrel. More seeds. Dan shook his head, and opened the third. A specter shot straight up from the barrel and hovered near the ceiling.

"Get behind me," I yelled.

"Why?" Dan asked as he raised his gun.

"You just freed a ghost."

The ghost slid against the ceiling from one wall to the next, a spectral version of pacing. I picked up the barrel's lid and smelled it; cinnamon and sage. Someone had worked a half-assed binding spell and trapped this ghost in a barrel of apple seeds.

"Can you hear me?" I asked. The ghost stilled, and I got a better look at it. He was a fiftyish man wearing high-quality clothes and shoes. In other words, his wardrobe didn't match my wardrobe.

"What's it doing?" Dan asked.

"Not it. He." Dan frowned, his gaze moving wildly around the room. I realized that I had one chance to prove that everything I'd told him was true, so I took off my watch and pushed up my sleeve.

"Give me your hand." He did, and I pressed his palm to the seer's mark on my inner wrist. Dan stared at my hand holding his against my skin, then he looked up and almost jumped out of his skin.

"Holy shit!"

"I take it that worked."

"How is this even possible?"

"It's because you're touching my seer's mark." Before I could explain the ghost rushed at me.

"You let a mere mortal touch your mark?" he demanded. He was so close I could count his crow's feet. "Helena would have been ashamed."

I went still. Helena was my grandmother's name. "Who are you?"

"Did oleander kill you?" Dan asked. I looked at Dan, wondering how he would have ever come up with that question. He gestured toward the ghost. "He's wearing the same outfit as our unattended death."

I turned back to the ghost. Dan was right; here was the spirit of the man who'd died in the kitchen on Suffolk Street. "If you knew my grandmother, you knew how to handle oleander," I said. "You were murdered."

The ghost sniffed. "I was, and it was ghastly."

"Death can be undignified." I looked around the almost empty, almost plain attic. "But, why are you here?"

"Hang on," Dan said as he broke contact with me and took out his phone. While he attended to his investigation, I moved to the side. The ghost moved with me.

"You knew my grandmother?" I asked.

"Everyone knew Helena," he replied. "She was the most powerful seer in generations."

"But how do you know me?" I pressed. "We've never met."

"You look exactly like Helena did when she was younger," he replied. "I know what happened to you. We all do, in my circles. I'm surprised you came back to the area."

I moved so my back was to Dan, and whispered, "Don't say that when he can hear you, okay?"

The ghost nodded. "Very well. Have you arrived to solve my murder?"

"Depends. Are you Jacob Allwood?"

"In the," he gestured toward himself, "not-flesh." I opened my mouth, but Jacob gestured behind me. "Careful. The mortal returns."

"Got the property records on the oleander house," Dan began, then he looked around. "Is he still here?"

"He is." I held out my wrist. Dan grasped my arm, laying his palm flat against my seer's mark.

"Do you two do this often?" Jacob asked, glancing between Dan and me. "Interesting."

"If you must know, it's our first time," I said. "You were saying, about property records?"

"What?" Dan asked, bewildered. "Oh, Right. Sorry, you're the first ghost I've ever met. Anyway, the house where your body was found, fifty-four Suffolk Street, is owned by a company called Suffolk Street Corporation. Does that company have any relation to this orchard?"

"Why are you asking me?" Jacob countered. "I didn't live there."

"No, but you did die there." I looked around the almost empty attic. "When was this orchard last in business?"

"Decades ago," Jacob replied. "I believe bell bottoms were in style."

"Do you know who killed you?" Dan asked. "Or who's in the cider vat?"

"If I knew who killed me I'd be making their life a living hell," Jacob spat. "And I didn't even know there was a cider vat on the property." Jacob paused. "Others approach."

"Detective Lyons?" someone called up the stairs.

"I'm up here," Dan yelled back. "Attic's empty. Be down in a sec."

I heard feet shuffling around the first floor, then the exterior door closed. When I looked back, Jacob was gone.

"Think he'll come back?" Dan asked.

"Depends on how mad he is." I shook out my wrist, but didn't put my watch back on. My skin was tingling where Dan had touched it, my mark hot. "A witch as powerful as he was can do a lot of damage, living or dead."

Dan shook his head. "We just talked to a ghost."

"I do it all the time." I descended the stairs.

"Got any other superpowers I need to know about?"

"I don't have any superpowers."

"After what I just saw, I beg to differ." Dan held open the door for me. I walked out of the farm stand into a gaggle of officers staring at us.

"Where are we at, folks?" Dan asked, either oblivious or uncaring about the officer's open curiosity.

"We're ready to cordon off the area and get the samples back to the lab," the forensics person, Jill, said. "Did you find any evidence in there?"

"No, but I did get an anonymous tip about that unattended death," Dan replied. "Our deceased party appears to be one Jacob Allwood."

Jill blinked. "You figured that out in a random apple orchard?"

"Yeah, it was carved on an apple." When Jill frowned, Dan said, "Someone called it in. Let's run that name, see what we can find."

"On it." Jill made a few notes, then she headed toward her vehicle.

Dan turned to me, and said, "Since you found the remains, I need to take a formal statement from you. Want to head down to the station now and get it over with?"

"Sure." I really didn't want to go to the police station on that or any other day, but I understood there wasn't a way around it. If Dan needed a statement, he would hound me until he got one.

"Fantastic. I'm driving."

CHAPTER 10

ROAD TRIP

DAN DID INDEED DRIVE to the station, which meant that when we arrived everyone inside got to gawk at me getting out of his car. Despite what Dan said about him not knowing anything about my past, I couldn't shake the feeling that most of his coworkers either knew all about my history, or they had some strong suspicions. I didn't want Dan to be labeled as the weird cop because he associated with me.

"When did you come to this area?" I asked. Dan cocked an eyebrow, so I elaborated, "I don't remember you from when I was younger."

"I moved here about seven, eight years ago," he replied. "Were you not around here, then?"

"No. I left for a few years."

Dan held the front door open for me, and we entered the station. It had a linoleum floor, mint green walls, and office furniture that looked to be twenty years old. If this place was supposed to strike fear into the hearts of criminals, it missed the mark.

"Wait here." Dan pointed at a desk, then he wandered toward a wall of file cabinets. I sat at the desk, barely resisting the urge to put my feet up.

Forensics Jill approached me and sat on the edge of the desk. "First Lyons starts driving you around, now you get his desk?"

"This is his?" I scanned the desk. It was a mess, heaped with pens and folders and other paperwork. "Will he get in trouble if I sit here?"

"No, no," she said, waving away my concerns. "It's just nice to see him open up to someone. He's been through some pretty dark times."

"He has?" My gaze found Dan across the room, scowling at a file. "He seems pretty happy-go-lucky to me."

"Around you, maybe. Around us, not so much."

Jill left to do whatever she did when she wasn't alluding to her coworker's past traumas, and I thought about what Dan had said in the farm store's attic. He'd said that he could tell someone had hurt me, and that he now had my back. At the time, I thought he was trying to gain my confidence, or possibly even flirt a little, but maybe wasn't that at all. Maybe his damaged soul recognized the damage in mine.

Now that's just silly.

Dan returned from the land of file cabinets, legal pad and voice recorder in hand. "Ready?"

"As I'll ever be."

I followed him into the same room he'd interviewed me in after the incident at the retirement home. The room held a table, two chairs, an analog clock on the wall, and nothing else. Fun times. Dan set the recorder on the table and turned it on.

"This is Detective Daniel Lyons interviewing Eliza Moore about an incident that occurred at Stone Creek Orchard," he began, and through his questions and my answers, we pieced together how and why I'd been in the barn and found the skull.

When we got to the part in the farm store's attic, Dan shut off the recorder. "What did Allwood mean when he asked if we did that often?"

"He was referring to me letting you touch my seer's mark," I replied. "Letting someone see a ghost that way doesn't always work. Usually you need some kind of connection."

"Connection," Dan repeated. "Well, we were working together."

"Yeah. We were." My phone pinged. I turned it over and saw an email from Bennet.

"Bennet just sent me the resume Nick used to get the job at the college." I angled my phone so Dan could read the document with me.

"So he claimed to have a bachelor's degree in horticulture, a few greenhouse jobs under his belt, and that's it," Dan said. "I wonder if he was honest about anything on here. Send me a copy?"

"You got it." I forwarded the email to his phone. Dan got the notification, opened it, and frowned.

"Who's T. Beauclaire? They're copied on this email."

"Oh, that's Tessa. Bennet's been copying her on all the emails he sends me. He claims she's much more organized than I am."

Dan glanced up from his phone. "Tessa's more than just your assistant, isn't she?"

"I trust her with my life." I slid my phone into my pocket. "What do you think the chances are of Nick and Jada Allwood being related to Jacob Allwood?"

Dan's eyes widened. "It's a leap. Allwood's a common name."

"It is, but I reviewed the property records and the land Nick's house is sitting on used to be owned by witches from the Allwood clan."

"How do you know they were witches and not regular people named Allwood?" I gave him a look. "Okay, then. In that case, I'd say chances are good."

"If we're done here, I'll head to the library and hit up the genealogy room. I'd like to dig into these Allwoods a little further."

Dan leaned closer and asked, "Couldn't you just ask Jacob whatever you wanted to know?"

"I could, but he'd either have to return to me, or I would have to summon him."

"You can do that?"

"Yeah, but I'd rather not. If he's moved on, I'd like to let him rest."

"Look at you, the ghost whisperer with a heart." Dan made a few notes on the bottom of the legal pad. "The way I see it, we could do one of two things. I could bring you back to your car, and you could go to the library."

"Which is what I already said I'm going to do."

"Or," he continued, "we could hold off on the library for now, and check out the college Nick supposedly attended. It's about thirty minutes from here."

"What will that accomplish?"

"Maybe nothing, maybe something," he replied. "You in?"

I should have said no. I had plenty of things to do, and I did not need Dan running my day like he ran his investigations... But checking out the college was a good idea. After the way my tattoo had flared at Nick's touch, I was eager to learn anything I could about him.

"Let's do it."

***

"Have you ever met Jacob Allwood before today?" Dan asked. We were back in his black sport utility vehicle, listening to eighties glam metal while we sped through the countryside. As road trips went, this one wasn't bad.

"The first time I ever saw him was when he was dead at that kitchen table," I replied.

"But he knew your grandmother."

"Do you hear everything?" I glared at him out of the corner of my eye. "You're like a bat."

"What can I say. I've got good ears."

I slunk down in the seat. "A lot of people knew my grandmother." I remembered the afternoon teas and cocktail parties she used to host, how I'd get sent to bed but would sneak out of my room and watch everything from the second floor landing. Gran knew I was there, but as long as I stayed out of the way she didn't mention it.

"I don't remember him ever coming by Gran's, but that doesn't mean he didn't," I said. "He could have visited while I was at school. Do you have a cause of death on him?"

"The medical examiner's working on it." Dan steered around a curve in the road. "Odd, that he was found in a house he didn't live in."

"Think he was moved after death?"

"No. He died at that table. The questions are how, and why." We paused at a red light, and Dan's gaze slid toward me. "Tell me about these witch clans. Are they feuding, like the Hatfields and McCoys?"

Hands over my mouth and nose, someone chanting a spell so that even though I wasn't breathing, I wouldn't die. I shook my head and willed the memories away, and said, "They have grudges, but they don't overtly fight between clans. It's all sneaking and subterfuge."

"If a rival clan killed Allwood, what might that mean?"

"For people like you, nothing."

"People like me?"

"You know. Mortals." Dan gave me a look that said he wasn't buying what I was selling, then the light turned green and I was spared further judgment. "Witches have been having spats all around town pretty much since the beginning, and mortals haven't caught on yet."

"Is that because witches are sneaky, or because mortals are stupid?"

"Little of both, I guess."

"Are you mortal?"

"Are you asking if I'm immortal?" I countered. "I'm a seer by blood. I won't live forever, and if I chose to I could wield some rather spectacular magic. And I get to talk to dead people. Witches, on the other hand, have an entire magical hierarchy, and are focused on rituals and spellwork."

"You mean you choose not to wield magic?" Dan asked, because of course that was the fact he latched on to. "Why not?"

I turned toward the side window and stared at the town speeding by. "I didn't want anything to do with this life, but you can't escape what you are."

The car stopped moving. A moment later I realized that Dan had parked in the college's visitor parking lot.

"Listen, I'm sorry I brought you to Allwood's crime scene," Dan said. "Maybe if I hadn't done that your mystery client wouldn't have sent you to the orchard, but you're not in this too deep. I can bring you home and you can wash your hands of this."

"Thanks, but I can't. For one thing, Jacob knows I'm involved, which means that even if his clan doesn't know already, they'll know about me soon enough. I'll see this through."

Dan pocketed the keys. "You are one tough cookie."

"I don't really have a choice," I said as I exited the SUV. "When a witch decides they need a seer, they'll do anything to get one."

"Even your girl Tessa?"

"Tessa is a unique case." I looked at the college. It was larger than the one Bennet taught at, and concrete walkways led to stately brick buildings that reached toward the clouds. Everything was arranged around a tidy courtyard. I wondered if students got demerits for stepping on the grass.

"Ever been here before?" Dan asked.

"I didn't get to go to college." I refused to look at Dan, but I could feel the weight of his curiosity. When he remained silent, I asked, "Are you going to start your research in the administrative offices?"

"That was my plan. I want to see if I can get my hands on any of Allwood's records."

"Have fun. I'm going to find the horticulture department."

"Sounds like a plan." Dan headed toward the closest building. "I'll meet you there," he called over his shoulder.

We set off in different directions, me acting as if I had a clue where I was going. I'd never been here before, and I had no idea where the horticulture department might be, but that didn't matter. Being trapped in a car with Dan and his endless questions right after giving a statement at the police station had worn down my nerves. I needed to clear the cobwebs out of my head, and figure out my next move.

Over the past few days I'd revealed more to Dan than I'd revealed to anyone in years, maybe ever. There was something about his manner that kept drawing information out of me, and for the life of me I couldn't figure out how he was doing that. Was he really that good at interrogating people? I was one question away from giving him the store.

I found a bench, and despite really wanting to walk I sat. This part of campus was wooded, and the surrounding pine trees felt like old friends. I closed my eyes and sent out my awareness in all directions. There were no ghosts in the immediate area, which was a relief. I fished my witchfinder out of my pocket, and found it cold. That meant the only supernatural human in the area was me, which was just the way I liked it. I tilted my head back, and concentrated on the sound of the wind rusting among the pines.

"Eli."

I opened my eyes, blinking at the bright sunlight. Dan was standing over me. "What time is it?"

"About an hour after we parked. How was the horticulture department?"

"I-I never found it."

"Not surprising, since it got shut down a few years ago." Dan sat next to me and set a stack of paper on my lap. "Those are some articles about its closure. What's more, no one with the name Allwood has ever attended this school."

"He really lied about his credentials, all of them," I said. I figured some of them had to be legitimate for Nick to get hired. "That also means that Bennet's college never checked his references. That seems like a pretty big oversight."

"What are the odds of Nick being a witch?" Dan asked.

"I don't know if that's the answer," I said. "And whether he is or not, Jada was still possessed. I think we need to figure out who or what possessed her."

"I'm starting to think you're on to something with the possible Nick-Jada-Jacob connection. If you don't mind, I'll also follow up on it."

"What will your department say about that?"

"If doing so leads me to figuring out who killed Jacob Allwood, they'll say great job." Dan stood and offered me his hand. "Come on. We got what we needed here."

During the walk back to the parking lot all I could think about was Nick. Why would he have lied about his education? I understood that he needed the job in order to get to me, but lying on his resume was an awfully big risk that could have easily backfired. Then again, Nick had been desperate to help his sister. My dad always said a desperate man was capable of causing all sorts of damage.

I briefly wondered if my tattoo had flared because of Nick's lie, then dismissed that idea. If the tattoo detected lies—and I didn't even know if it could do that—Nick would have had to been lying as he kissed me... But, what does one lie about while mid-kiss? Having a girlfriend, or maybe a wife? Then again, that didn't make sense either. He'd been Jada's caretaker for twenty years, and I didn't think a possessed sister was conducive to dating. There was also the kiss itself; Nick's lips had been soft, hesitant at first, as if he was waiting to—

"Earth to Eli," Dan said.

"What?" I asked, then I realized we'd reached his car. Worse, I was standing there reliving my and Nick's kiss instead of getting in the car.

"Sorry," I said as I got in the passenger side. "I was thinking about the case."

"You're mind's probably wandering because you're hungry. We've been at this all day."

"Yeah. Maybe."

"Let's grab a bite. I'll buy you dinner."

"Dan. I can't go out to dinner with you."

"Why not?"

"Because we're working a case together. What we have is a professional relationship, nothing more."

"I agree that we're both professionals, however I eat with my coworkers all the time."

"Where? In the police cafeteria?"

There was that look again, the face he probably thought was scary. "Since you don't want to eat with me, you don't get to find out."

"That's fine. I keep granola bars in my glove box."

When we reached the orchard, the sun had started to set. Even though there was still plenty of light, the orchard was definitely more foreboding than it had been that morning.

"We're here," Dan announced. "Enjoy your granola."

I put my hand on the door handle, and paused. "Thanks for helping me. I know this is way outside your comfort zone."

Dan shrugged. "A case is a case. When I get more information, I'll call you."

"Thanks. I'll do the same."

With that Dan drove off and left me alone in an orchard with a headful of questions, and no idea of where to find the answers.

Chapter 11

Tangentially Related

After Dan dropped me off at my car, I returned to my apartment and went through my usual nighttime routine. I did the dishes, sorted my mail, and swept the waiting room floor. We hadn't had any clients stop by in a few days, so the public portion of my apartment was pretty clean. That was too bad, since nothing cleared my head as well as an epic bout of rage cleaning.

I sat at my desk, powered up my laptop, and stared at the screen. So much had happened over the past few days, and I needed to figure out what was related to what. It couldn't all be connected, could it?

Good grief, I hoped not.

I called up a blank document and listed everything that had happened with Nick and Jada, beginning with the incident in the third grade and ending when Nick touched one of my protection tattoos. That was a year's worth of drama in itself, but now I had to deal with a random death due to oleander poisoning, the skeleton in the cider vat, and Jacob Allwood's well dressed and recently freed from an apple barrel's ghost. Nope, that wasn't a lot to worry about. Not at all.

The cursor blinked impatiently while I stared at the screen. The potential complexity of the events I'd listed hinged on one specific fact: were Nick and Jada Allwood somehow related to Jacob Allwood?

Since the blank page wasn't offering any answers, I did the next best thing and called Nick.

"Hello?"

"Hey, Nick. It's Eli."

"Oh, Eliza, about what happened—"

"It's okay." I didn't know if he wanted to apologize for kissing me like a sailor on shore leave or for my tattoo's warning shock, and at that moment I didn't care. "Can I ask you a question about your family?"

"Certainly. I fear you already know our darkest secret."

We would just see about that. "I know you said your family is English, but are you in any way descended from the local Allwoods?"

"Funny you should mention that. There is an ancestor—I'm not certain how far back she is; at least a few hundred years—who was called Sarah Allwood. Family legend says she was run out of town for feeding children poisoned apples, like an old hag in a fairy tale."

"Yeah, just like. Is she the only Allwood you know of?"

"No, she's not. From what I understand after the incidents in question, the majority of the family moved out of the area, thus distancing themselves from the scandal."

"Smart." I thought about Nick's dulcet tones, and that smooth British accent. "Why do you have an accent?"

"I'm sorry?"

"You're from here, yet you have a British accent. Why is that?"

Nick cleared his throat. When he continued, all traces of Britishness were gone. "I've spent a great deal of time abroad. I speak that way out of habit, not to deceive anyone."

"Good to know. Thanks for your help!"

I ended the call before he could say anything further. So everyone was related, tangentially at least. That meant that both Nick and Jada were descended from witches, but did they know that? From what Nick said the apple poisoning had been a rather mundane event, if it had even occurred at all. But if he wasn't witchborn, why had my tattoo warned me to get away from him?

There was only one person who knew exactly why and how my tattoo would activate, and that was the man who'd given it to me. I sent an email to Dad, asking him for a list of reasons why the tattoo would warn me. I didn't know where he was, or when he would be able to check his email, but I knew he would get back to me. My father had never let me down.

I closed my laptop, shut off my lamp, and went to bed. Hopefully I would be able to find an answer for at least one of my many questions tomorrow.

Chapter 12

WHEN I WAS SEVENTEEN

I COULDN'T SLEEP WHEN a case remained unsolved, which sucked. As soon as my alarm went off the next morning, I gave up on sleep and went out for a run. I hadn't made it a mile before my phone buzzed. I checked the screen. Dan was calling me.

It wasn't even seven in the morning, and Dan was calling me.

I accepted the call and said, "Do you ever sleep?"

"Like a baby," he replied. "We verified that the body found at the unattended death is in fact Jacob Allwood, not that you and I had any doubts. We don't have a cause of death yet, but I've got news about your skull." He paused. "Why are you panting?"

"I was running. Tell me about the skull."

"Female, elderly, and old."

"Elderly and old? Does that mean she was extra old?"

"It means this female died a long time ago, and she was elderly when her death occurred. We're reaching out to the university's archeology department, but the current guess it that the skull is a few hundred years old."

"A few hundred? Like, maybe four hundred years old, there-abouts?"

"That's a very specific question. What do you know?"

"I think that skull belongs to Sarah Allwood."

I heard papers rustling. "Where are you?"

I rattled off the cross streets. "Why?"

"I have questions, and I don't think this is something we should talk about on the phone or at the station. I'm coming to get you."

Dan ended the call. I was still staring at my phone when he pulled up and opened the passenger door for me. "That was fast."

"I was at the diner. Want to talk at your place?"

"Sounds like a plan."

We completed the short ride back to my building, then Dan parked and followed me up the back stairs. Dan is carrying his phone and paperwork.

"Want to hit the coffee shop?" he asked.

"I have coffee." I unlocked the door, and Dan followed me into the kitchen. "Have a seat," I said as I put grounds in the coffeemaker and poured water into the reservoir. Once it was brewing, I faced Dan.

"There's cereal and bananas on the counter, and milk in the fridge. Help yourself. I'm going to change."

I left him contemplating the finer points of breakfast cereal and disappeared into my bedroom. I pulled off my sweaty running shirt and decided to hop in the shower. I made it quick, and five minutes later I joined Dan in the kitchen. I poured myself a mug of coffee and sat across from him at the table.

"So, what's all this?" I asked.

"It's a bunch of facts, and they don't add up." He glanced up, his gaze lingering on my wet hair. "You showered?"

"You are perceptive." I tugged some of the papers toward me. "Tell me these facts."

"Stone Creek Orchard has been closed down since the early seventies," he began. "The owner is listed as a Jacob Allwood, who, as you know, is deceased." Dan met my gaze. "I ran Allwood's net worth. It is astronomical."

"That's not unusual." I went to my desk and grabbed a notebook and pen, and wrote down what Dan had told me. "Witches know how to extend their life span. The longer you live, the more wealth you accumulate. Oh, Nick and Jada are definitely related to the Allwoods."

"Where'd you find that?"

"I called Nick and asked him."

"At least you didn't fall into the trap of going to his place again. Alone."

"Are you ever going to let me live that down?"

"Nope." Dan got up to refill his coffee. While his back was turned I took a moment to appreciate the tight black tee he was wearing. It did a great job of showing off his muscular arms and back. Tessa was right; Officer Muscleman worked out.

"Are you working today? You look awful casual," I added, jerking my chin toward his jeans.

"It's my day off."

"If it's your day off why are you swimming in case files? Take some time for yourself, relax a bit."

Dan reclaimed his seat across from me. "I don't have much else to do. You get it."

"I do?"

"What do you do on a day off? Don't tell me you leave all this behind."

"It's different for me. I was born into this." I picked at the corner of the file folder. "Besides, I tried leaving it all behind. It didn't work."

Dan placed his hand on top of mine. "I'm sorry."

The front door opened. I slid my hand out from under Dan's, trying to ignore the loss of warmth.

"Good morning," Tessa called. She breezed into the kitchen carrying a bag of groceries, and smiled when she saw Dan. "Detective Lyons, what a surprise! Did you sleep over?"

"He did not," I said. "He's working on his day off."

Tessa gave Dan a look. "Everyone needs time off."

"I know, I know," he said. "Maybe I just missed you, Tess."

Tessa's smile returned. "Eli Jayne, you could take a lesson from this man. Flattery is a very useful tool."

"Anyway," I said, glaring at both of them for good measure, "Dan's got some news, and I have a hunch. You'd better sit."

Tessa left the bag on the counter and sat. "I'm all ears."

I indicated Dan should go first. "The skeleton Eli found at Stone Creek Orchard turned out to be female, and very old," Dan began. "The good news is that it doesn't appear to be a homicide, at least not a recent one."

"And the bad news," Tessa prompted.

Dan gestured to me. "Not bad, so much as interesting," I began. "First of all, Jacob Allwood's ghost was in the farm store. He'd been trapped there with a binding spell."

"Oh, my," Tessa said. "Had he been dead long?"

"Near as we can tell, only a few days," Dan replied. "Someone poisoned him with oleander, and left his body in a house he didn't live in."

Tessa's lips flattened. "Go on."

I took a deep breath, and went for broke. "I think the skeleton is—was—Sarah Allwood."

Tessa's eyes widened and she shook her head. "Eli, are you sure? That... That would be very bad, especially for you."

"Why for Eli?" Dan asked. "What could a long dead woman do to her?"

Tessa didn't look at Dan as she replied. "Sarah Allwood was a powerful matriarch, and she was the meanest woman you ever met...but it's her daughter, and her son in law, you need to be worried about."

"I don't follow."

"Sarah Allwood's daughter, Jemima, married Nathaniel Beauclaire."

"Oh." I sat back against the chair, feeling like all the air had rushed out of my lungs. "The ghost that possessed Jada was called Nathaniel."

"Beauclaire," Dan said. "Isn't that your name, Tessa?"

"It is," she replied. "It's also—" She paused, and said, "Eli, if this is really going all the way back to Sarah Allwood you should tell him."

"Tell me what?" Dan demanded.

"You wondered why I never went to college," I began. "I wanted to. I really did. But when I was seventeen..."

I coughed and looked away. It shouldn't be so hard to talk about this, not eleven years afterward. "When I was seventeen I was kidnapped by the Beauclaire witches and held in their basement for..." I glanced at Tessa. "Three weeks?"

She nodded. "Yes, about three weeks."

Dan turned to Tessa. "Your clan kidnapped Eli?"

"My clan had nothing to do with it," Tessa replied. "A few rogue offshoots decided they needed a seer, and in their infinite stupidity thought that kidnapping Eli was the best course of action. When I found out I went straight to Helena and told her everything."

"Your grandmother rescued you?"

"No. My dad and Tessa did." I remembered the basement door flinging open, and my father standing at the top of the stairs with Tessa right behind him.

"Alexander razed that house to the ground," Tessa said, a note of admiration in her voice. "He made sure no Beauclaire would be foolish enough to go near Eli."

"Except you," I said.

"Well. I'm not really a Beauclaire. I married into the clan."

"You're married?" Dan asked,

"I was. It was a political marriage. All marriages were, back then."

"Royalty still marries for politics and alliances," I pointed out.

"Wait." Dan looked at Tessa for a moment, then said, "You're telling me you're a witch that married into royalty."

"No, silly," Tessa said. "I am royalty by birth, and my then-husband married into my family. I also happen to be a witch."

"Tessa is short for Contessa," I added.

"Now we've got royalty," Dan muttered. "Let's get back to Eli. What happened after you were rescued? Did these kidnappers go to jail, hopefully for a long time?"

"They were turned over to the clan elders for punishment," Tessa said. "Even I don't know what happened to them."

"They just disappeared," I said. "And now you know why I have a hundred protection tattoos. Dad made sure no one could ever take me against my will ever again."

"Good man," Dan said, then he frowned. "Why did they take you, specifically?"

I opened my mouth to reply, but no sound came out. It was as if my throat had had enough remembering and decided to close up. I grabbed my mug, and ran my thumb along the smooth curve of the handle until I could speak again.

"I'm out of coffee," I mumbled, then I got up and filled my mug. Once that was done I walked out of the kitchen and onto my balcony. I stood there, feeling the cold air on my skin and the hot mug in my hands, and let my mind go blank. That had always been my defense mechanism when life got too heavy, to concentrate on whatever physical sensations were present and let everything else fall away. It was what I had done when I was trapped in that basement; I'd been there so long I'd lost hope, but instead of giving in to despair I concentrated on my environment. It was the only thing that kept me sane, and it had helped me figure out how to escape.

I heard the sliding door open and shut behind me, then Dan stood beside me.

"Great view."

"Yeah." I pointed eastward. "That's Knob Hill. I used to hike up there all the time."

"There are some great trails thirty, maybe forty minutes north. If you're still into hiking."

"I am. Did Tessa tell you what happened?"

"She did not. She said the rest isn't her story to tell."

I smiled into my mug, saw my reflection in the dark liquid. "That is a very Tessa thing to say." We stood together in silence for a few minutes, and I debated not telling Dan anything about my kidnapping, but that wouldn't be fair. More people were involved than just me. A man was dead, a woman had been possessed, and for all I knew everything was related. Witches have long memories, and eleven years isn't too long to hold onto a grudge.

"I told you that most ghosts have better things to do than harass the living, and that's true," I began. "However, some witches—not most witches by any means, but some—believe that they can wield more power after death than they can while still alive."

Dan grunted. "Is that true?"

"Theoretically, yes. It would require a huge amount of preparation, and people who remain loyal to the witch long after their death. It's like an Egyptian pharaoh's death cult, where they have a temple built and worshippers leave offerings. Only with these clans, it's your descendants that take care of you."

"Exactly how do you care for the ghost of a witch?" Dan asked.

"That's more of a question for Tessa." I set my mug on the railing, and told him what he really wanted to know. "When I was kidnapped, they wanted the spirit in question to possess me. There's a myth that if a seer is possessed by a witch's spirit, the spirit/seer combo becomes immensely powerful and can direct the actions of other ghosts."

"They wanted you to help them raise a ghost army."

"Yeah."

"Unlucky for them, you're too tough for that."

"That's the thing. I wasn't tough. They stripped me and beat me and left me down there, for days all I did was cry—"

"Hey. Hey." Dan grabbed my shoulders and turned me toward him. "Cut yourself some slack. You were a kid, scared and alone." He frowned. "Were you alone?"

"Yeah. Mostly." I wiped my cheeks with my palms, then I linked my hands behind my neck. "I wasn't tough, but I was smart. I didn't know where I was, but I was on a dirt floor. I listened to the earth, figured out where I was, and then I got a message to Tessa. Sending her that information almost killed me. I half thought I would die before she found me, but even if I had died my body would have been evidence. Evidence enough for whoever found me to figure out what had happened. "

"How did you send the message?"

"Astral projection. My gran taught me." I stared at the clouds. Others saw shapes in the sky, but I never had. I only ever saw clouds. "I only projected to Tessa because she's a witch, and witches had taken me. I had no idea they were from her clan."

"You did the right thing."

"I guess." I looked Dan in the eye for the first time since he'd come out to the balcony. "Now you know."

"Now I know." He paused, then asked, "Who did they want to possess you?"

"I don't know. They never said the ghost's name around me. If they ever admitted it afterward, no one told me."

"Do you think Jacob Allwood wants to possess someone?"

I shook my head. "I think someone wanted to take him out of the picture. His ghost was trapped in that attic. If we hadn't gone upstairs and opened that barrel he would still be in there." I took a deep breath. "Maybe I should summon him. Back at the orchard, he didn't seem to know who killed him."

"With oleander, no less." Dan grabbed his phone and thumbed through a few screens. "We're still working on notifying the family. None of them have been interviewed yet. Would they talk to you about witch business? Would they talk to Tessa?"

"I'd rather not get Tessa involved. She really stuck her neck out for me in the aftermath of all that, and she was almost banished for it. I need to keep her as far away from this mess as possible."

"Understood." Dan pocketed his phone. "I'll see which family members I can get at the station. Once everything's set up, I'll let you in on the dates and times."

"Thank you. And, Dan," I added, when he moved to go back inside, "Thanks for not making me feel like a victim. Thank you for listening."

"You're welcome, but you were wrong about one thing. You said you weren't tough, but you were smart. Being smart is the first step to being tough. If you can't out fight the bad guys, you've got to out-think them."

"Okay. I accept your logic."

He grabbed his chest. "Was that a compliment? I'll hold it next to my heart for all time."

"Come on, you goof. We have a case to crack."

Chapter 13

Who Wanted Your Spirit?

Dan left soon after my balcony confessional. The workaholic was going in to the station on his day off to set up interviews with however many Allwoods would talk to us. While I went over my notes about the case, Tessa unloaded her groceries into my cabinets.

"What'd you bring me this time?" I asked. I'd long since stopped trying to repay Tessa for the various supplies she brought me. I wasn't kidding when I told Dan that a witch's longer than average life meant they could amass a substantial amount of wealth, and Tessa was no exception. Therefore, Tessa had money to burn.

There was also the fact that Tessa still felt a tremendous amount of guilt about what had happened to me. She hadn't been involved in my kidnapping, but members of her clan had abducted me. That had hurt her deeply. If bringing over a few tins of cookies helped assuage her guilt, I was all for it.

"Oh, the usual. A bouquet of flowers and some candy for the bowl up front, and snacks for us." Tessa set a plate of artfully arranged cookies on the table. A moment later, she brought over a teapot and two cups. Most wouldn't follow their morning coffee with a pot of Earl Grey, but not Tessa and I. We could caffeinate like champs.

"I'm surprised you didn't bust out the good cookies for Dan," I said as I grabbed one. "Or are you saving those for Bennet?"

"I don't need baked goods in order to acquire a partner," Tessa said as she poured the tea. "You, however, need all the help you can get. When did you last have a significant other?"

I narrowed my eyes at Tess. She knew exactly how long it had been since I had a boyfriend, and why I hadn't had one since. "Anyway. Let's talk about something other than my lack of a love life."

"All right. Did you tell Dan everything?"

"Not everything." I hadn't even scratched the surface about what I'd endured during those three weeks of hell. "I told him enough."

"How did he react?"

"He was surprisingly calm." I don't know how I'd expected Dan to react to my admittedly abridged version of being abducted and held captive for weeks in a cold, dark basement, but I definitely hadn't expected him to listen without judgement while I told my story.

"That's good. It's a rare person who can listen objectively to such an account."

"Speaking of rare people," I began, desperate to change the subject, "tell me about Jacob Allwood."

"He's an elder," Tessa said. "The Allwoods aren't as strong as they once were, but then again, most clans are a shadow of their former selves. Even so, Jacob was very old, and he wielded a great deal of power."

"Was he as old as you?"

"No, but he was more powerful. For someone to get close enough to murder him and move his body ..." Tessa shook her head. "Let's just say I'd rather not meet that individual."

I grabbed a third cookie. I hadn't eaten after my run and I was starved. "Do you think we should summon him and find out what he knows about his death, or will it just piss him off?"

"If he has half a brain he'll understand we're trying to help him."
Tessa stood and walked toward the supply closet. "I'll get the candles."

***

Summoning a ghost is rather easy. All you have to do is clear your mind of distractions, and then focus on the decedent in question. That's right, almost every fortune teller and séance facilitator out there is hawking snake oil when they drag out their cards and crystal balls. You can use those items for other forms of magic, but ghosts tend to ignore all of that. Once you leave the material plane behind, all those props are just so much clutter.

My gran had begun training me to summon when I was a kid. It began as our daily meditation practice; five minutes when I first woke up, and five minutes before bed. Eventually those five minutes became two hours of meditation and mind work per day, and by the time I was twelve—the age when most seer abilities manifested—I could summon individuals who had died decades before I was born. Of course, my abilities had a head start, since the incident with Jada had forced them to manifest when I was eight.

And now, I would use them to summon a witch elder.

Tessa set a candle in the middle of the table while I closed the curtains. A candle was a traditional tool to help one focus, and I did not need any nosy neighbors peeking in on my séance. Not to mention, it was much easier to see a ghost in the dark. Direct light tended to shine right through them and bleach them out. Any time a spirit was in the same room as I was, I wanted to know exactly where they were.

Windows covered, I went to my herb cabinet and selected a branch of dried oleander. I sat across from Tessa, and set the oleander next to the candle.

"Going for broke?" she asked, jerking her chin toward the oleander.

"If you're going to do it, do it all the way." I snapped my fingers and the candle's wick ignited. "Let's do it."

"I'm here."

Twenty years' worth of experience with ghosts sneaking up on me meant I outwardly didn't react to Jacob's sudden appearance. Inwardly, I was screaming like a banshee.

Jacob Allwood's ghost was seated to my right. He seemed calmer than he'd been at the orchard, not that I had any idea how a ghost should feel after getting freed from a confinement in an apple barrel . His shirt also seemed different, which was interesting. Altering your appearance isn't something newbie spirits were known to do.

"Hello," I said. "I wasn't sure you would come."

"I don't have much else to do," he replied. "Being dead is rather boring." Jacob turned his attention to Tessa. "I see you've brought a witch."

"Actually, I was already here," Tessa said. "I'd say it's good to see you, but under the circumstances I don't know if that's appropriate."

"Always proper, Ms. Beauclaire," Jacob said. "Even polite in your betrayals."

Tessa smiled. "I'd be offended, but my abundance of life force reminds me that I am in a better place."

"That's enough," I said; I had no idea how strong Jacob's spirit was, and I didn't want him to waste energy bickering with Tessa before I got my questions in. "You can insult each other later. Jacob, when we found you at the orchard you were rather disoriented."

"You would be too, if you'd been trapped in a gods-forsaken barrel for such a long time."

"According to forensics you only died a few days ago."

"My last living memories are of preparing for the clan's Yule celebration," Jacob said.

I glanced at Tessa, and she shook her head slightly. Neither of us had expected that tidbit of information. "Do you remember how you died?"

He cast a ghostly hand toward the oleander. "I don't. I don't remember anything until you freed me." He tried to grasp the branch, and frowned when his hand passed through it. "I do know it wasn't oleander that did me in."

"Are you sure? Where your body was found—"

"Why wasn't I at home?" he demanded.

"I don't know." He gestured for me to continue. "You were sitting at the kitchen table wearing the same clothes your spirit had on when we met at the orchard." I paused, wondering how much detail I should give him. "I was at the scene. Your hands had the sort of rash you'd get from improperly handling oleander."

"But that's the thing, I know how to handle oleander," he said. "I can handle all the major poisons. I was a master before Helena was even born."

I pursed my lips; I did not like how he kept mentioning my grandmother. "Who wanted you dead?"

He laughed through his nose. "Many people."

"Who wanted your spirit?" Tessa asked, which was a much better question. "Some person or persons went through the trouble of separating your spirit from your body, then they kept that body alive for four months. That's an awful lot of work, just to dump your body in a random house and sprinkle it with oleander."

"The house wasn't random," he said, then he paused. "Four months?"

"Yeah. It's April."

Jacob clenched his fist so hard his knuckles showed white. "That—this—is unacceptable. I am the clan's elder. For someone to violate my body and my spirit, there will be consequences."

"There will be," I said. "Help us find who out did this to you."

Jacob glanced around. "Is your mortal here? He's the one with insight into my predicament."

Tessa's brow pinched. "You have a mortal? Does he mean Dan?"

"Dan asked Jacob a few salient questions at the orchard," I replied, hoping she would drop it. "The mortal is currently rounding up your clan for questioning. Anyone in particular he should talk to?"

"My sister, Cecily," Jacob replied. "She'll know what happened. Cecily always knows."

"I will pass that along. What do you know about a Nathaniel?"

Jacob stared at me as if I'd grown a second head, then he turned to Tessa. "Is she serious?"

"As a heart attack," Tessa replied. "Won't oleander induce a heart attack?"

Jacob ignored Tessa's last comment, and said to me, "The only Nathaniel I am aware of is Nathaniel Beauclaire, and you'd do well to stay far away from him."

"No arguments there," I said. "We think his spirit possessed a girl for the past twenty-odd years."

Jacob shook his head. "Impossible. As of this past Yule, Nathaniel was still alive."

I stared at Jacob, feeling as if the floor had fallen out from under me. "You're certain?"

"I am." Jacob's gaze slid toward Tessa. "Surely you were aware of this."

"I cut ties with the Beauclaire's after they abducted Eli," Tessa said. "Doing so was a condition of my freedom."

I blinked; I never knew that. "Where is Nathaniel now? Or where was he this past Yule?"

"As far as I know he returned to the old country," Jacob replied, "and we should hope he remains there. Nathaniel is a prime example of what happens when we isolate ourselves within our power. He had no one to say no to him, and that has led him to put in motion some truly mad plans."

"So he's a villain surrounded by sycophants." I leaned back in my chair. "Great."

"This is no trivial matter," Jacob snapped. "Nathaniel is much older than I am, and much more powerful. He seeks to return to the way things were, when witches and even seers wielded more power than mortals."

I tapped my fingers on the table. "Is that why you're," I gestured toward his noncorporeal form, "like this?"

"Perhaps. I was known for standing in his way." Jacob turned back to Tessa. "As were you. Surely you would stand in his way again."

"I would," Tessa said. "Will you help us stop him?"

"I will, as long as you find whoever did this to me."

Tessa met my gaze. I nodded. "We will," I said. "I will have Dan contact your sister so we can talk to her. In the meantime, do you know what Nathaniel wants?"

"What he's always wanted. An army." With that bombshell, Jacob dissipated.

"Well, he was either out of energy or had someplace to be," Tessa said.

"There were conditions for you to remain free?" I demanded.

Tessa sat back in her chair. "There were. The seer community was up in arms after you were abducted, more so after you were found. Many called for harsh punishments to the entire clan, even those who weren't aware of what had happened… and the other clans agreed. They didn't want their good names besmirched by what the Beau-claires had done."

"But the entire clan wasn't punished," I said. "Why were you? You saved me!"

"But I knew where to find you," Tessa said. "It's unusual for some-one as young as you were to astral project with such clarity. It was said that you hadn't projected to me, but that instead I was a party to your abduction."

"But you weren't!" My hands were shaking, so I sat on them. "Were you?"

"No. No! Eliza, I was not!" Tessa moved to the chair beside me and held my face in her hands. "Eliza, I would never harm you. I hope you can believe me."

"I do." Tessa squeezed her eyes shut and rested her forehead against mine. "Were you cast out of your clan?"

"Not hardly," Tessa said as she released me. "They lauded me as a hero. I was their poster child for good witches, and the reason why we shouldn't all be punished."

"What did Gran say?"

"She said they should make me the head of the clan and I should dole out punishment to the guilty parties as I saw fit."

"And Dad?"

"He thought those responsible should be slowly, painfully, and publicly executed." Tessa smiled. "I've always gotten along with Alexander."

I shuddered; sometimes I forgot Tessa was from an older, bloodier era. "So why did you cut ties?"

"It was a compromise, but one that I chose. I am to stay away from the Beauclaire's for the rest of your natural life, and as long as I do no seer will seek vengeance against me."

I bit my lip. "Thank you."

"You are very welcome. I like you better than those moldy old witches, anyway." Tessa blew out the candle, then she rose and started opening the curtains. "We have much better adventures."

I picked up the dried branch of oleander. Jacob was adamant that he understood how to handle oleander, and that his last memories were around Yule. How had he died? Where had his body been since last December? And how had his spirit ended up trapped in the orchard?

"I have a feeling this adventure will be one for the books," I said, twirling the branch in my fingers.

"No doubt about that."

Chapter 14

Three Ghostly Cats

After Tessa and I cleaned up the kitchen, she left to run a few errands while I took a drive to the other side of town to water Gran's plants. I needed time to clear my head, and let's face it, those plants weren't going to water themselves.

I never knew that Tessa had been accused of being part of my kidnapping, or that she'd had to cut ties with her clan in order to remain unpunished. In the chaotic aftermath of my rescue, I was busy recovering, and I'd never really thought about what had happened to her. Once I was well enough to travel, and Dad was due for his next assignment, Gran had encouraged me to go with him so I could leave the whole situation behind.

I spent the next year traveling with my father, and when I returned home, I spent a bare week with Gran before Tessa stopped by and asked if I'd like to accompany her on a trip. She and I traveled together off and on until a little more than a year ago, when Gran got sick.

Sometimes I miss my gran so much I don't know what to do with myself

But today wasn't one of those days. I had tasks to complete, and I would do them.

I pulled into the driveway and looked up at Gran's massive Victorian house. She'd been adamant that despite its grand appearance and many rooms, it wasn't a mansion. "A mansion is something people buy for appearances," she'd say. "This is a home for our family." I couldn't argue with that, even though these days it was only a home for three ghostly cats.

"I'm home," I called out from the mudroom. Not a minute later I heard the patter of three sets of paws, and the Feline Federation came to greet me. They were called Smokey, Pumpkin, and Muffuletta, a gray, calico, and tabby cat. These three had been with Gran since she was a kid, and when they passed on, she somehow brought their spirits back in such a solid state, they looked and behaved like living cats. We'd all assumed they were tied to Gran and they would follow her once she passed, but she was gone and here they remained. I hoped Gran didn't miss them too much.

"I missed you, too," I said, as I crouched down to hand out the obligatory pets and scritches. After they were placated—for now—Pumpkin hopped onto my shoulder and I went into the kitchen to fill the watering can. That done, I opened up the solarium.

I have a feeling that when Bennet ordered his authentic Victorian greenhouse, he'd been trying to copy Gran's solarium. This room predated the Victorians by a few decades, but it was magnificent. It was a hexagonal room set right off the kitchen, and the first few plants inside the door were culinary herbs. Go a few steps further in, and that's where the edibles ended.

Gran had loved her plants, and most of all she'd loved her poisons. The biggest and oldest plant was a white oleander, which my grandfather, Adesh, had given her on their wedding day. He'd definitely known the way to Gran's heart. Also present were several species of lilies, some foxgloves and hyacinths, and a huge purple-flowered thornapple. Despite that almost everything in this room could kill me, it was my favorite spot in the house.

Watering complete, I flopped down onto one of the three chaises Gran had arranged in a circle. Honestly, in the year since she died I'd changed nothing about the house, and I had no plans to. It was perfect the way it was.

Pumpkin reentered the solarium and hopped onto the bookcase. She's always been my favorite of the Feline Federation, originally because she was a calico. I loved her orange spots, shaped like tiny pumpkins on her back. As I got older I realized that Pumpkin has a sixth sense about her, and she frequently saw answers where others saw obstacles. I approached the bookshelf, and her fluffy tail brushed the spine of a certain book: Granny Apple's Magical Recipes from the Orchard.

"Where did this come from?" I'd read every single book and pamphlet and reference material in this house at least twice, and I had no memory of an apple-based cookbook. I flipped to the title page, and saw the author listed as Granny Apple. Cute, in a nauseating way. The publisher was Stone Creek Press.

Jacob Allwood's ghost had been trapped in a barrel of apple seeds at Stone Creek Orchard.

"Thanks, Pumpkin." I scratched her ears, and slid the cookbook into my bag, planning to read it back at my place. Since everything was as it should be, I returned the watering can to the kitchen, gave the Feline Federation their goodbye snuggles, and locked up the house. These days I didn't mind leaving the house empty, not like I had right after Gran died. The cats would keep watch, and I'd be back in a few days, anyway.

I stepped onto the side porch and swept my gaze down the street. Kid me had loved living here; I would ride my bike down the wide avenue, climb the gnarled old trees, and do all the carefree things a kid is supposed to do. After I'd spent eight stifling years being ignored by my mother, coming to Gran's house was like heaven. For nine perfect, happy years, my life was good.

Now, my life was good again. It wasn't perfect, but that's the secret of life: nothing's perfect. But when you've got a safe place to sleep, food in your kitchen, and people that care about you, life is good. Although Tessa was right, I hadn't had a boyfriend in a while. Not that I would ever admit to her that I thought she was right, especially since she got it into her head that Dan and I were a match. I could not see myself dating a cop, not in this or any life.

I spied movement at the top of the street; a man had turned the corner and was walking toward the house. Even at this distance I could see he was tall with golden blond hair, and he was carrying some paper bags from the market two blocks over. I wondered if he'd picked up a few things for dinner, and if his significant other was waiting for him. Maybe there was a bottle of wine sitting on the counter, just waiting for him to pour it, or a cake baking for dessert. It was something I used to do all the time, fantasizing about other people's lives. Tessa would say my voyeurism was why I became a private investigator. Dad would have called me curious, and repeated his saying about a curious mind being the greatest tool one could have.

Curiosity overtaking propriety, I moved to the front of the porch to get a better look at the man, and did a double take. Of all people, Nick Allwood was walking toward my grandmother's house.

That's right, he lives nearby. I didn't remember seeing a car in his driveway, and this neighborhood is within walking distance from the college he worked at with Bennet. Since he hadn't noticed me, I kept up my spying. Gotta call it what it is, right? As I watched him walk down the street, I was struck by how attractive he was. Add to that his intelligence, the good conversations we'd had, and that when he kissed me, I'd kissed him back. Dammit, I wanted to get to know him better, but my stupid tattoo had sent a warning shock.

Let's see if it shocks us again. Leaving all common sense on the porch, I bounded down the steps and onto the sidewalk. Nick halted when he saw me, looking as if he'd seen a ghost.

"Miss Moore," he said, then he looked at the house behind me, clearly wondering what I was doing in his neighborhood. "I was not expecting to see you."

"I was at my gran's, watering the plants." I jerked my chin toward the bags. "Need a hand?"

"They're not heavy, but thank you," he replied. "Would you like to walk with me?"

"Sure."

We set off toward Nick's place. "How's Jada doing?"

"Much better. The doctors hope she'll be able to transition to a group home soon. If she does well there, she'll be able to come home."

"That's great."

"About what happened at your office," Nick began. "I apologize if I was too forward."

"It's okay. You just surprised me."

"Was it a good surprise?"

I felt my cheeks warm. "Yeah. It was."

I glanced at Nick, saw him smiling. Maybe he was just a guy with an unfortunate family situation, and that was what the warning was about. I could definitely see my tattoos warning me off from a man close to a possession.

"And, when I touched your leg," he continued.

"That must have been static electricity, or something," I said quickly. No reason to run off the cute mortal.

"Or something." We turned the corner and were at Nick's place. "I would invite you in, but I'm not set for company."

"It's okay. Thanks for the walk."

"It was a good walk." We smiled at each other.

"Well, I'll be seeing you."

"Of course." I turned to walk back to my car, when Nick said, "Miss Moore!"

I turned back. "Yeah?"

"Perhaps, when we next see each other, you'll allow me to buy you dinner."

"Only if you call me Eli instead of Miss Moore."

Nick smiled, and that shock of golden hair fell over his eyes. "Very well, Eli. I will call you to arrange a date?"

"I'll be waiting."

Nick caught my hand and raised it to his mouth. "As shall I," he said, then he kissed my hand.

I turned to go, grinning so hard my cheeks hurt. The cute boy asked me out. My life was definitely good.

CHAPTER 15

WHOA WHOA WHOA

THE NEXT MORNING, I went for a run. I'd just gotten into my running groove when Dan called me, because of course he did.

"Do you have an alarm set to call me as soon as the sun comes up?" I asked, in lieu of a proper greeting.

"That's a great idea. I'll set that up for tomorrow." When I didn't respond, he continued, "I've got some Allwoods coming in to talk this afternoon."

"Is Cecily among them?"

"She is." Dan paused. "Want to tell me why you're interested in her?"

"Tessa and I summoned Jacob's spirit," I began. "He told us we should talk to Cecily. He said she would know what's up, and he said some other things, too." I looked up, saw people walking toward me, and turned away from them. They probably weren't involved with our case, but I couldn't be certain. "I'll tell you when I see you."

"Want me to pick you up?"

"No. I'll meet you at the station."

"Sounds like a plan."

I ended the call and shoved my phone in my pocket, brushing my witchfinder as I did so. It was hot enough to scorch me.

I didn't look back at the people approaching me on the sidewalk. Instead, I ran.

After my abduction, I'd thought everyone was after me. Understandable, right? But I couldn't live that way. I had to get on with my life, but every time I saw an unfamiliar face I worried they were a Beauclaire lackey sent to watch me and wait for me to slip up. Wait until they could take me again, and finish what the others had started. After a few months of dealing with my paranoia, Tessa gave me my witchfinder. It was a silver amulet on a black silk cord, and it was designed to warm up whenever a witch was close by. It worked perfectly, as did all of Tessa's spells. The amulet gave me peace of mind, and let me venture out into the world again.

That amulet was now so hot it could burn a hole in my jacket.

I didn't know if any of the people on the street were witches, or if they were inside the shops, or if they were watching me. I didn't even know if anyone was following me, or if I'd crossed paths with a few innocent witches going about their business. What I did know was that I'd been talking to the recently deceased head of the Allwood clan, I might have stepped in Beauclaire business, and I wasn't going to let anyone take me again.

I took a circuitous route that looped through a few parking lots and doubled back several times. When I finally got back to my place, I was exhausted and drenched in sweat. I locked the door, closed all the curtains, and called Dan.

"Lyons."

"Can you come to me?"

"Where are you?"

"My place. Someone might have been following me."

"Be there in five."

"Door's locked. I need to shower. There's a key above the door-frame."

"Got it."

Dan ended the call. I set my phone down on the kitchen table and made a beeline for the bathroom. I left my running clothes in a heap on the floor, turned the water up as hot as it would go, and got in. I was still standing under water when I heard footsteps in my apartment.

"Who's there?" I yelled.

"It's me," came Dan's voice. I pulled the shower curtain aside and saw him standing in the bathroom's doorway. He has his back to me and his gun raised.

"Apartment's clear," he continued. "I wasn't followed. I'll wait in the kitchen."

I watched him reach back and shut the door, then I slithered to the floor of the tub and pulled my knees up to my chest. My heart was hammering against my ribs, and my breath came in ragged gasps. Goddamnit, I couldn't live like this. I'd been doing so well—so well!—and now I was reverting back to a terrified seventeen-year-old. I needed to pull myself together, solve this case, and send teenager Eli back to the past where she belonged.

The water went cold before I'd calmed myself down, which sucked. I turned off the spray, put on my robe, and went out to the kitchen.

Dan was sitting at the kitchen table facing the door. His gun was back in its shoulder holster, and he had another set of case files spread out in front of him. Since I was barefoot he didn't hear me approach. I sat across from him and said, "Thanks for getting here so fast."

"Like I said, I've got your back." He looked up, and raised his eyebrows at my robe and soaked hair. I was too rattled to care about things like pants and dripping on the table. As if he'd never seen a woman in a bathrobe before. "What happened?"

"I was running, and my witchfinder went off."

"Witchfinder?"

"Yeah. Tessa made it." I pulled it out of my robe's pocket and set it on the table. I'd brought it into the shower with me, just in case. "If a witch is near it heats up."

Dan eyed the amulet. "May I?"

"Sure."

He picked it up, and turned it over in his hands. "When did it heat up?"

"Right after we hung up, just before seven."

"You didn't call me until an hour later."

"I know. I-I was trying to lose them."

Dan set down the amulet and took my hands in his. "Next time, call me the second this thing heats up. We'll lose them together."

I nodded, not trusting my voice. The coffee maker beeped, and Dan rose and poured two mugs. When he came back to the table and set one in front of me, I just stared at it.

"Don't look so shocked. I'm good with small appliances." He went to the fridge, and came back with the milk. "You should see me make toast."

"I don't know what's wrong with me." I picked up the milk, only to set it down again. My hands were trembling and I didn't trust myself to pour it without making a mess. "I'm around witches all the time. It's no big deal. But earlier, my witchfinder went hot and I ran."

"Maybe your instincts took over for a good reason." Dan added the perfect amount of milk to my coffee. I took a sip, and let the caffeine soak into my bones and make me feel like a human again.

"I'm sorry I pulled you away from your work."

"The office is boring. Why do you think I'm always game for checking out apple orchards and college admissions offices?" He smiled, and something about his square jaw and warm brown eyes put me at ease.

For all that he drove me nuts, Dan exuded goodness. How he'd ever ended up hanging around with me was a mystery.

"You were going to tell me what else Allwood revealed yesterday," he prompted, reminding me that we were, in fact, working.

"First off, Jacob's last living memories were from December," I began. "He was overseeing the clan's Yule preparations. Then, bam! It's four months later and we find his spirit trapped at the orchard."

"Wait, does that mean he was incapacitated for four months, like in a coma?"

"Not necessarily. I think someone separated his spirit from his body, and kept his body alive for... Well, I don't know why."

"Did they want someone to possess him, like what happened to Jada Allwood?"

I set my mug down so hard coffee sloshed up and over the rim. "That's it," I said as I mopped up coffee with my sleeve. "Tessa and I thought someone wanted his spirit, but it must have been his body they were after. Possess the head of a powerful enough clan, and the world's your oyster."

"Wouldn't the people around him know he was possessed?"

"Not necessarily. If the entity possessing the body knows the person in question—"

"The possessee?"

In spite of everything, I smiled. "Yeah. If the entity knows the possessee, or if they're a good enough actor, that entity could ride a person's body for a long, long time." I thought about Jada, and wondered if she would ever understand what had happened to her. "The only way a possession's really ever detected is if the entity outs itself, or if those who know the possessed one catch on."

Dan shook his head. "Sounds heavy."

"It is."

"Did Jacob say anything about his place of death?" Dan asked. "That wasn't his house."

"He said the house wasn't random, then he dissipated. Spirits, especially newer ones, can't sustain communication with the living for very long. Hang on."

I went to my desk and grabbed my notes from the day before. When I turned back to the table I saw Dan eyeing my robe. "Sorry about this," I said, gesturing at my state of dress.

"It's fine," he demurred. "I just hope you're planning on putting something more on before we go to the station."

"What time are the interviews?"

"No one's coming in until three. We have time." He jerked his chin toward my notes. "What have you got there?"

"Jacob mentioned that Nathaniel Beauclaire is still alive. I'm wondering how he fits in to all of this."

"The same Nathaniel Beauclaire that married Jemima Allwood?" Dan shuffled through his folder, then he pulled out a blurry photocopy. "According to this, they were married in sixteen forty-two."

I sat and pulled the paper toward me. It was a photocopy of a handwritten ledger. "Where'd you get this?"

"I called the library. They've got all sorts of information." Dan scratched a few things onto his notebook. "Is it weird that a couple of witches got married in a church?"

"Oh, definitely. Usually they drape an altar in black and sacrifice a baby to celebrate their unholy union."

Dan set down his pencil. "I know this is all old hat for you, but I only ask questions when I don't know the answer."

And, I felt like a jerk. Dan consistently went out of his way to help me—hell, he was putting his job on the line by even believing me—and I couldn't bring myself to drop the attitude.

"Sorry," I said. "I was trying to be funny. I guess I'm not."

"You are, sometimes." I peeked at his face, saw him smiling. "Okay, usually you're funny."

"Good to know," I said, borrowing one of his lines. "As for the marriage, it would have been weird if they weren't married in a church. Just like Tessa said, marriage is more about combining assets and consolidating power than anything else. They needed the paperwork to make it legal."

Dan shook his head. "And here I thought you were supposed to marry for love."

I snorted. "That only happens in fairy tales."

Dan watched me for a moment, and I steeled myself for his inevitable defense of marriage and true love. He surprised me by bringing the conversation back to the case.

"I am glad that no babies were harmed in the making of this marriage," he said. "Would this Nathaniel really still be alive?"

I shrugged. "Witches live a long time. I don't see why not."

"A long time." Dan's forehead creased like an accordion. "How long are we talking?"

"A few centuries isn't out of the ordinary."

"Wait. If witches live for such a long time where are all the witch children? Why aren't the schools packed with little kids doing magic?"

"Fun fact, those of a supernatural bent are much less fertile than mortal humans. Supernatural children come along much less frequently than mortal kids."

"What about seers? Are you looking at another few hundred years on this rock?"

I turned my attention to my notes. "At this rate I'm not sure if I'll hit thirty." I stared at the photocopy for another moment, then I grabbed my phone.

"Who are you calling?" Dan asked.

"Bennet. Shepherd's keep all sorts of records." I put the phone on speaker mode and set it in the middle of the table. It only rang twice before Bennet picked up.

"Good morning, Eliza."

"Hey, Bennet. Dan's here with me."

"Yo."

"Ah. Yo to you, as well, Detective. What can I do for you?"

"What do you know about Sarah Allwood, and Nathaniel Beauclaire?"

"Oh. Um. That's a rather oddly specific request. What did Tessa have to say?"

"I'd rather not ask her." Out of the corner of my eye, I saw Dan raise an eyebrow. I ignored him, and said, "Conflict of interest, and all."

"Yes, well. As I'm sure you're aware, Nathaniel Beauclaire is a witch of some renown. He's frequently touted as an ideal warrior, and is said to have fought in several significant battles; the Somme, Agincourt, Hastings—"

"Whoa whoa whoa," Dan interjected. "The Battle of Hastings, as in William the Conqueror?"

"Why, yes. Is there another Battle of Hastings I should be aware of?"

Dan sat back against the chair, mind visibly blown. "We're good," I said into the phone. "Just making sure we're all on the same page."

"Good, good. After amassing quite an empire in England, Beauclaire came to this country when the courts first began sentencing criminals to transportation. He surmised, rightly so, that the colonies were rife with cheap labor."

"Beauclaire's rich and old," Dan said. "What do you know about Sarah Allwood?"

"Also old, but not nearly as wealthy," Bennet replied. "As far as I know she's also been deceased for quite some time. I will have to double check the dates, but she's been gone for several hundred years."

"But Nathaniel is still alive."

"Yes. I believe so."

I tapped the point of my pencil against my notebook. "What are the odds of the Nathaniel that possessed Jada being Nathaniel Beauclaire?"

"Very low, I'd say. Jada was possessed for what, twenty years? That would be a very long time for Beauclaire to possess her. His own body would deteriorate in the interim, possibly beyond repair."

"How long could he have possessed her, without damaging his own body?" Dan asked. "A few months, maybe?"

"Perhaps, but even that would require a vast amount of resources. I would find it more likely that Jada was possessed by a spirit that had no body to return to."

"Like Sarah Allwood," I said. Dan nodded and scribbled something down. "Bennet, can you do some research on these lovely folks and get back to me."

"Of course. I should have something for you by the end of the day, or perhaps tomorrow."

"Thanks."

Bennet ended the call. I glanced up, saw Dan furiously making notes. "What are you thinking?"

"You didn't ask Carrington to do the research. You told him." Dan fixed me with his gaze. "Does he work for you?"

"It's complicated." I got up and went to the cabinets to get a cereal bowl. "Hungry? I only have healthy cereal. I'm out of the good stuff."

"I'm good. So shepherds are lower than seers. Are they lower than witches?" He paused, then asked, "Seers are the ones calling the shots, aren't they?"

I paused with my hand on the cereal box, unnerved but unsurprised that Dan had parsed that bit of hierarchy all on his own. "When my gran, Helena Moore, was alive she was the matriarch of the seers."

"Of the seers in this area?"

"No. Of all of them." I poured cereal into my bowl, and returned to the table. "Anyway, Bennet seems to have a hard time accepting that a Moore isn't in charge."

"Why aren't you in charge?" I decided to add milk to my cereal instead of answering him. "Okay, if you're not in charge who is?"

I shrugged. "My dad, maybe? I try to stay out of it."

"Maybe you should get back in it. For one thing, all evidence points to people being after you."

The cereal turned to sawdust in my mouth. "How so?"

"When the entity first possessed Jada when you two were kids, it was aiming at you."

I cleared my throat. "We don't know that."

"It said so back at Allwood's. Then a mystery client sends you to the orchard, where we find a skull and a witch's trapped spirit. Add to these facts that everything keeps pointing toward a Nathaniel, there is a Nathaniel Beauclaire out there, and that you have a history with Beauclaires, and it's pretty obvious."

"It's not," I protested, albeit weakly. "I get sent after weird spirits all the time. You're new to all this, but it's what a seer does. Really."

"I may be new to your world, but facts are facts. Follow them long enough, and they lead you to answers."

I stabbed the cereal with my spoon. "Yeah. Okay. You have a point there."

"So." Dan leaned back in his chair and linked his arms behind his head. "What are we going to do about it?"

"We?"

"Allwood's death is my case, remember? I'm in this just as much as you are."

I swirled my spoon around my very mushy cereal. There was no way I could eat this. "I guess you are. So, what's our next move, detective?"

"Let's go back to the orchard."

"The place where a crazy old woman made poisoned apple pies and a witch was trapped in a barrel," I said. "Why not? What could go wrong?"

Dan leaned forward and said, "What was that about poisoned pies?"

Chapter 16

Cecily

I GOT DRESSED WHILE Dan loaded the dishwasher, then we went straight to Stone Creek Orchard. He drove, not that he'd asked if I wanted to. I got the feeling that after my morning freak out, Dan wasn't letting me out of his sight. For once, I was okay with his babysitting.

I also brought along Granny Apple's evil cookbook. Actually, from what I'd read, the cookbook didn't seem evil at all, just full of homey old-fashioned desserts, although that made it even more suspicious. My gran hadn't been known for her baking, but she did know how to quickly and quietly poison an enemy.

When we reached the orchard, Dan drove past the parking area and right up to the crest of the hill. From that vantage point, we could see the trees and barn spread out below us.

"What did the investigators find in the barn?" I asked. It was the first time either of us had spoken since we got in the car.

"An enormous amount of rotted fruit, and enough bones to make up one human skeleton." Dan drummed his fingers on the steering wheel. "Makes you wonder what we're missing."

"Maybe we haven't missed anything. Maybe we haven't found it yet." My phone buzzed in my pocket. I set the open cookbook on the dashboard, withdrew my phone, and saw a text from Nick.

Nick: Dinner tonight?

Eli: Maybe. Need to wrap up a work thing.

Nick: Tomorrow, then?

Eli: Ok. Talk soon.

I shoved my phone in my pocket. "Sorry."

"Don't be. For you to smile like that, it must have been good news."

I glanced in the side mirror. I was smiling, and dammit, I liked smiling. Then I remembered all the unanswered questions and loose ends swirling around Nick, and it faded.

"Did you ever look into why Nick lied about his credentials?" I asked, trying and probably failing to sound nonchalant.

"Nah. Lots of people lie on their resumes. The kid probably just needed a job."

"Why did you call him a kid? You can't be much older than him."

Dan's gaze slid toward me. "You think?"

"Well, I'm not going to card you. Want to look around the barn again?" Suddenly, the interior of the car was too small for me.

"Sure."

We walked toward the barn, me leading the way. I cut through the orchard. The trees were still laden with perfectly ripe, perfectly out of season fruit.

"Why did an anonymous neighbor want me to come here?" I asked the trees. "The neighbor specifically mentioned letting the apples rot so the farmer—whoever that is—can strain out the seeds. But, there is no farmer." I stepped closer to a branch and scrutinized the fruit. "So, who was hoarding those barrels of apple seeds?"

"Could be it's like you said, and someone wanted the cyanide."

I shook my head. "Getting cyanide from apple seeds is time-con-suming and expensive. You have to crush them and mix in certain enzymes, then wait for the cyanide to crystalize. It's a fun experiment, but it's not practical." I frowned, remembering the age of the skeleton I'd found. A few hundred years ago mashing up apple seeds might have been the most efficient way to extract cyanide.

"You and I have different ideas of fun."

I glanced over my shoulder at him, but he wasn't looking at me. I followed his gaze, and saw it fixed on the barn. "I guess we do."

"Then we still don't know why anyone was hoarding these seeds in the first place. I still think it was to plant trees, like Johnny Appleseed."

"But, you don't grow apples from seeds. It's just not done... Unless, this is an older operation than we realized."

"As in, these trees were planted before grafting was a thing?"

"Not before grafting, but maybe by someone who didn't know how to graft. Maybe someone just needed a ton of apples and planting them from seed was the best way for them to do it." I placed my palm flat against a trunk, wishing the tree could share its memories with me. "Even if that's the case, we still don't know who tends the orchard now. Would they really still need to hoard seeds?"

Dan whipped out his phone and typed something in. "You also don't let the apples rot to get the seeds," he said. "The seeds would rot, too."

"Curiouser and curiouser." I picked an apple, testing its weight. "But some neighbor was upset enough by all this to contact me." I whirled around and faced Dan. "Who called in the wellbeing check for Suffolk Street?"

Dan shrugged. "Neighbor," he replied, then his face lit with recognition. He raised his phone to his ear; a moment later I realized he was calling the station.

"It's Lyons. Do we have a transcript of the wellbeing call for Suffolk Street?" He paused. "Really. Well, someone must have called it in. Why else would we go out there?" Another pause. "Okay. Thanks."

He slid his phone into his pocket. "There's no records of anyone calling the station about a missing neighbor."

"Odds are it was the same individual that was concerned about this orchard." I threw the apple as far as I could, and watched it sail over the treetops before it fell back to earth. First, Dan gets a call about an unattended death while he's having coffee with me, and we find Jacob Allwood's body. Then, I get a case that takes me to Stone Creek Orchard, and we find Jacob Allwood's spirit. I reached a single, inevitable, awful conclusion.

"You're right. This is all pointing toward me."

"Do you know why?"

"No... But Jacob keeps mentioning my grandmother. When we freed him he knew who I was. He said I looked just like her when she was younger."

"Was your grandmother pretty?"

"She was beautiful." I thought back to the second time I'd spoken to Jacob. "He mentioned her when we summoned him, too. I wonder if this has something to do with Gran."

"But, isn't she gone?"

"Yeah. She is." I closed my eyes and took a breath. I would not summon Gran for help. I would figure this out on my own.

"Let's go talk to Cecily, and the rest of the Allwoods."

"Sounds good."

We walked back to the car. "Sorry we skipped the barn."

"Don't be. I've seen enough of this place for one lifetime."

"I bet." We reached the car, and something occurred to me. "Why did you ask if my gran was pretty?"

"Because you said you look like her."

With that, Dan got in the car. A moment later I followed suit, fully intending to ignore that last comment, when the cookbook caught my eye. I'd left it open but upside down on the dashboard, with a drawing of an autumn dessert table laden with pies and a bouquet spread across the pages. Upside down, it was something else.

"Dan, look."

He glanced at the cookbook, then at the orchard spread before us. "This drawing is a map," he said. Using his finger he traced the conspicuously blank areas through what were cookies on the page, but trees in the orchard. At the end of the path was a glorious pie. Its real world counterpart was the barn.

"X marks the spot," he said. "What was the treasure? The bones?"

"I don't know," I said. "I don't know if I want to find out, either."

***

During the drive to the police station I paged through the cookbook, pausing at every drawing and examining them from all angles. Every single one of them appeared to be a fruit- or baking-based sketch. Then again, the dessert table scape hadn't looked like anything other than what it presented as, until I saw it laid out next to the orchard.

"Find anything?" Dan asked.

"A recipe for peach cobbler." I closed the book and contemplated flinging it out the window. "Why would anyone hide maps in a dessert cookbook?"

"Beats me. You found that at your grandmother's house?"

"Technically, Pumpkin found it."

"Pumpkin?"

"One of the cats. Her tail brushed—"

"You mean to tell me you leave pets closed up in that house, all alone?"

The way Dan was scowling I worried he was going to call animal control. "It's okay. They're ghosts."

Dan's scowl was replaced by a blank stare. "Of course they are. Do you know any living people?"

"I know you."

He didn't respond to that. A moment later we pulled into the police station's parking lot, and Dan said, "Here's the thing, I can't let you sit in on the interviews."

"I figured," I said. "I can hang out in the waiting area until they're done."

"I tried to get you consultant status, but that didn't work out."

"I thought police consultants only happened on television." We got out of the car and entered through the station's side door. "Like on that show where the devil's a detective."

"I love that show. Also, I want his wardrobe." I followed Dan to his desk, which looked like it was about to collapse under the amount of paperwork. The stack in the inbox was dangerously listing to the side.

"Maybe you should get a secretary," I said. "Tessa likes you, and she's very organized."

"I thought she was busy with Carrington," Dan said, then Jill, the forensic investigator, approached us.

"One of your interviewees is here," Jill said. "I've never seen anyone so eager to spill her guts."

Dan glanced at the clock on the wall. "She is four hours early."

"Actually, she was five hours early," Jill said. "She's been waiting, impatiently, and insists she won't talk without her present."

"Her?"

Jill indicated me. "She said, and I quote, if that Moore girl isn't present I'm not answering a single question."

"Let me guess, this person is Cecily Allwood?" I asked.

"I see you've had the pleasure," Jill said.

"Not yet, but I've heard plenty." I glanced toward the front desk. "Why are you on desk duty?"

"Desk sergeant's sick." Jill turned to Dan. "Should I send Ms. Allwood in?"

Dan grabbed a legal pad and a few pens. "Might as well start now. I guess you're in, Eli."

I watched Jill return to the waiting area and direct Cecily toward the interview room. "Great."

***

Cecily Allwood was an almost exact copy of her brother, with the exception of her not being dead. She wore the same well-tailored, expensive yet bland clothing, high-end leather pumps that carried her soundlessly across the linoleum floors, and her barely used designer bag probably cost more than my monthly rent. Her face was smooth and unlined, and her blonde hair was pulled back into a perfect chignon.

It was her hairstyle that betrayed her true age and marked her as someone not of the modern era. No one wore chignons anymore.

"Ms. Allwood, I'm Detective Lyons," Dan began. "Thank you for coming down today. My condolences on the loss of your brother."

"Thank you," Cecily said, then she speared me with her gaze. "You're Eliza Moore?"

"I am," I replied. "If you don't mind my asking, why did you want me here during the interview?"

"In matters of the uncanny a seer's input is always desired," she replied.

Dan's gaze slid toward me, then he asked, "When did you last see Jacob alive?"

Cecily glanced at me. "I last saw him a week ago."

"You mean you saw his body," I said. "When did you last have a conversation with him?"

Cecily pursed her lips. Apparently my input was desired, but not my questions. "December."

"He was found in a house that he didn't live in, alone and with no identification," Dan said. "The place is owned by the Suffolk Street Corporation. Know anything about that?"

"Yes. We own that corporation. Surely you knew that?"

"Surely you knew about the trail of shell companies that made tracking down the true owners of the company very, very difficult," Dan countered. "But that's beside the point. Was Jacob staying there?" When Cecily didn't respond, Dan continued, "Don't you want to know what happened to your brother?"

"She already knows," I said. "Jacob said you knew everything."

"Did he?" Cecily demanded, then her eyes widened. "You've spoken to him."

"I have, and he stated in no uncertain terms that you were the one with information about his death."

"Well, he was wrong." Cecily clasped and unclasped her hands. "Shortly before Yule, Jacob fell ill. It was nothing out of the ordinary, and nothing we couldn't counteract. Jacob decided to go out while he was healing, but his spirit never returned to us."

"Go out?" Dan asked.

"Astral projection," I replied. To Cecily, I asked, "When did you realize his spirit was in jeopardy?"

"By the time the new year began it was clear that something had gone terribly wrong. I didn't know what to do, but I also didn't want it common knowledge that Jacob was out with his body left vulnerable. I kept him sequestered at home with around the clock care, and waited for him to return." Cecily faced me. "Do you know where he was? His spirit, that is?"

"I do. Detective Lyons and I freed him from a barrel of apple seeds."

Recognition lit her eyes. "He was at the orchard?"

"Yes," I replied, not hiding my surprise. After my last conversation with Jacob I'd assumed he had visited his sister. "You really didn't know that?"

"What about his body?" Dan asked. "How did he get to Suffolk Street?"

"And what about the oleander?" I added.

Cecily shook her head. "I don't know the answer to either of those questions."

Dan and I glanced at each other, then he said, "You mean to tell me that someone infiltrated one of the most secure compounds on the east coast, made off with the clan head's body, and you don't know how it happened?"

"That is correct."

"Wow." I had majorly screwed up a few times, but I'd never done anything like this. "Do you have a lot of security failures, or were you saving up for this one?"

Cecily's eyes flashed as she clenched her fist. "Young lady, I will not have you insulting me!"

Dan raised his hands. "No magic in the station, unless you want a building full of cops to know you're a witch."

She flattened her hand on the table. I saw a wisp of smoke escape through her fingers. I'd struck a nerve. "Forgive me," Cecily said. "I am terribly upset over the loss of Jacob."

Dan glanced between the two of us, then asked "Who's the head of the clan now? Are you in charge?"

Cecily swallowed hard. "No. Despite that I'm now the eldest the others would never support me. We will have to elect a new leader, but I doubt it will be me."

"Interesting." Dan made a few notes.

"How did Jacob die?" Cecily asked. "It wasn't really oleander, was it?"

"You're right. The oleander was just for show. Near as we can tell his body gave out." Dan flipped through his paperwork and made a few more notes. "Now that we know you had him under care, his body probably couldn't hold out once he was taken from home, and he was no longer getting that care."

Cecily squeezed her eyes shut. "I hope he wasn't in any pain."

"Why didn't you call the police when he went missing?" Dan asked.

"And say what? My brother, head of our clan of witches, sent his spirit out in December and now his body is gone, too?"

Dan shrugged. "We've gotten stranger calls."

"Why didn't you call me?" I asked. "I could have found him. In fact, I did find him."

"Because of your grandmother," Cecily replied. "Helena and Jacob had a history."

"Did they." I glanced at Dan, and shrugged. "It must have been several lifetimes ago. I never once heard my grandmother mention Jacob, or your clan."

"Seers and witches used to work much more... closely than they do today," Cecily said, letting the insinuation hang in the air. "Much like you and your mortal."

"Are you trying to provoke me by insulting my grandmother, or by suggesting that I have an inappropriate relationship with Detective Lyons?" I countered. "As barbs go, that's pretty lame. I've been insulted by much wittier people than you."

"What she's doing is wasting our time," Dan said. "Usually when a suspect lowers themselves to casual insults they're trying to shift the blame from themselves. Think she offed her brother?"

"I wouldn't put it past her."

"Stop talking about me as if I'm not here," Cecily snapped. "I am not a suspect!"

"Actually, you are," Dan said. "You freely admit that your brother needed medical attention, yet you didn't bring him to the hospital. That same incapacitated man went missing, of which you admit you were aware of, and you didn't call the police. Now, he's dead." Dan set a pair of handcuffs on the table. "Sounds a lot like murder to me."

"I did not kill Jacob," Cecily shrieked. "You can ask him yourself!"

Dan laughed shortly. "No, ma'am, I can't. I don't talk to the dead like you people can."

"Just touch her mark, like you did before." Cecily sneered. "Filthy habit."

"Nice try," Dan said as he reached for the cuffs.

I put my hand on his arm. "Wait. She knows you touched my mark." I sized up Cecily's appearance. She didn't seem particularly strong, either physically or magically. "That only happened once."

Cecily's eyes widened and she clutched the armrests. Dan got up, went to the door and locked it. "She doesn't look like a runner, but you never know," he explained.

I clasped my hands together and leaned toward Cecily. "Dan has touched my mark exactly one time. That means you talked to Jacob after we did." I leaned closer, and continued, "Listen, don't mind Lyons. He's a mortal, you know? He doesn't get our community, how it works. I believe you. I don't think you killed Jacob."

Cecily visibly relaxed. "You don't?"

"Of course not. It wouldn't make any sense. But, I do think you're hiding something." I thought about Jacob's appearance, both his corpse and his spirit. "He wasn't really sick in December, was he?"

"No. He was given something to make him ill and then convinced to go out, so we could prepare for your possession."

I blinked. "My possession?"

"Yes. That's been the goal all along, to have the spirit that was trapped in the child leap into you."

"The child?" I repeated. "You mean Jada?"

"Like it was supposed to when they were kids," Dan said, and Cecily nodded.

"Exactly. The plan was to have Helena's grandchild possessed by one of ours. That way our clan could have a seer again, just like in the old days."

I swallowed hard. "Who possessed Jada? Was it Nathaniel Beauclaire?"

"Close, but no. It was his mother-in-law, Sarah Allwood."

***

I pushed open the side door, crossed the parking lot, and vomited into the bushes.

What happened to Jada in the third grade hadn't been a freak accident. None of this had been an accident. People had been hunting me my entire life, all because of how I'd been born.

It wasn't my fault I was a seer. It wasn't my fault I was Helena Moore's granddaughter. But goddammit, it will be my fault when I take these bastards down.

Dan found me about twenty minutes later, sitting on the ground with my back against a tree. "Is this tree poisonous?"

"It's an oak."

"That didn't answer my question."

"It's not poisonous." Dan held a water bottle in my field of vision. Great, he and probably the entire station had watched me puking.

"Thanks." I twisted open the bottle, and drank. It was ice cold, and for a moment I concentrated on the chill temperature. "Did Cecily tell you anything else?"

"Apparently, certain members of the Allwood clan have watched you since birth," Dan began. "When you started attending some kind of weekly kids meeting, Sarah's spirit was put into a vessel—"

"A mirror," I said softly. "She was trapped in a mirror."

Dan squeezed my forearm. "Yeah. A mirror. She was in there waiting for you, but missed the mark."

"You said certain members of the clan." I put my hand on top of Dan's. "So all the witches aren't after me?"

"She claims that Jacob was vehemently against any plan involving you," he replied. "She also claims she really doesn't know how Jacob's body was moved, but suspects it was by those who wanted to have his spirit return to his body. She doesn't think they were trying to kill him, but save you."

"You believe her?"

"For the moment. She's also agreed to hand over the compound's surveillance footage. I don't think we'll actually find anything, but I have to move in official channels."

"What did she unofficially tell you?"

"There is a history between her family and yours, but it goes back before Jacob. Apparently, Nathaniel Beauclaire's been pulling the strings behind the Allwoods for generations."

"Then he's the one who had a beef with Gran." I pulled my legs up to my chest and rested my forehead on my knees. "And now he has a beef with me."

"Do you know how your grandmother was involved with them?" Dan asked. "Jacob kept going on about how much you look like her. Is this a case of unrequited affection?"

"No. Maybe. Honestly, I don't know."

I heard Dan take a breath, then pause as if he was organizing his thoughts. "How does Tessa know your family?"

"Tessa's known us for—" I sat up faced Dan. Based on the multitude of creases on his forehead, we'd come to the same awful conclusion. "She's a Beauclaire. But—she's my friend." With trembling hands, I shoved my hair back from my face. "She's always been my friend."

"As far as we know she still is," Dan said. "Still, maybe we should be cautious around her, for now."

"Yeah." My thoughts spun out of control. I'd know Tessa for my entire life. Next to Gran, she was the closest thing to a mother I had. More than that, she was my protector, my confidant. She was my closest, dearest companion.

"Tessa knows literally everything about me," I said. "The only things she doesn't know are what's happened this morning."

Dan nodded. "Then we'll keep it that way, and keep our wits about us."

I leaned my head against the oak. "The oleander," I said, remembering the potted specimen conveniently placed near Jacob's body. "I know why they left the oleander near Jacob's body."

"Why's that?"

"It was my gran's favorite flower."

CHAPTER 17

SITUATIONS LIKE THIS REQUIRE BALLAST

WHILE DAN FINISHED UP with Cecily at the station, I walked home. Dan had offered to drive me, but I needed time with my thoughts, my memories of Gran and Tessa, and this weird ass cookbook.

I paused in front of a bakery and took in the decadent window display. There were cakes, fresh bread, piles of cookies, and some round pastry that might have been a sweet roll. Whatever it was, I needed it. Then I saw the cannolis and my stomach audibly growled. Maybe I should take Dan up on his offers to buy me lunch, propriety be damned. Chasing down witches and ghosts was hungry work.

As I salivated over the deserts, I thought about the cookbook tucked away in my bag. Why would someone hide a map in a sketch of a dessert table? Why hide one in a cookbook at all? Dan had alluded to the drawing being like a treasure map, and if he was right—and let's face it, Dan's instincts were always spot on—the treasure in question was in the barn. The forensics team had gone over the place with a fine-toothed comb, and the only out of the ordinary item they found was the skeleton in the cider vat.

The skeleton that may have once been Sarah Allwood.

Situations like this require ballast. I went inside the bakery and came out with a half dozen cannolis. Eating real food would have done a much better job of bolstering my brain power, but I hoped the sugar high would help me puzzle out some of the cookbook's secrets. Besides, I could always make a salad for dinner.

Back at my place, I set my laptop up at the kitchen table, then I hauled over my printer and plugged it in. For that, I ate cannoli number one. Once everything was powered up, I found an aerial map of Stone Creek Orchard and printed it, then I flipped to the sketch of the dessert table. Little by little, I lined up the landmarks on the map with the images in the cookbook; the platter of orderly hand pies represented the apple trees, the icebox cake was the farm store, and the pièce de résistance—a caramel apple pie—was the barn.

"Shit." I leaned back, astounded at the similarities between a sketch in cookbook and satellite photo of an orchard. "Dan was right."

I grabbed my second, well-earned cannoli and took a bite. I'd no sooner swallowed when I heard the front door, and Tessa's shoes click-clacking across the floor.

"Cannolis," she said, when she found me in the kitchen. "What's the occasion?"

"I was hungry and walked by a bakery." I replied. "Help yourself."

"I shall, after I make some tea." She opened the tea cabinet and started rooting around for a suitable blend. "What are you working on?"

"You'll never believe this, but I found a cookbook at Gran's with a map hidden inside."

Tessa went still. "What is the map of?"

"Stone Creek Orchard."

Tessa sat across from me. "May I?" she asked, and I slid the cookbook toward her. She looked over the cover, then flipped through a few pages. That done, she cracked the book's spine and laid it flat on the table and held her hand over it. The pages fluttered in a graceful arch before settling down again.

"What was all that?" I asked.

"I pulled out the ink that was used to conceal what was originally written," she replied. "This was at Helena's?"

"Yeah, right on the bookshelf in the solarium." I watched Tessa examine one page, and then turn to the next. "See anything you recognize?"

"No, but I suspect this is a ledger of sorts," she replied. "Instead of listing items of value, it has maps of where they're located. How did you figure out there were maps?"

"One of the pictures lined up with the orchard." I pointed toward the representation of the orchard's barn. "That's where the skeleton was in the cider vat. Think it was Sarah Allwood? In other news, it was Sarah Allwood who possessed Jada."

Tessa bit her lip. "Sarah has been dead for a long, long time. For her spirit to remain strong enough to possess someone, people—likely her descendants—must have been caring for her remains."

"I guess so." I watched as Tessa turned the page. "You don't seem surprised by any of this."

She sighed. "This isn't the first case of a rogue spirit I've encountered."

"You're not surprised by the book, either."

"Things have a way of turning up in Helena's house," Tessa replied. "It's been that way for as long as I've known her. What upset you?"

"I'm not upset!"

Tessa reached across the table and grasped my hand. "I found you sitting in the dark eating cannolis and searching for maps under pictures of pie. Talk to me, Eli."

"You won't like it."

"Tell me anyway."

"Dan and I talked to someone, and it seems that the Allwood witches have been after me my entire life, all because of some unrequited crush Nathaniel Beauclaire had on Gran." I raised my gaze to Tessa's. "Did you know about that?"

"Yes," she replied. "Nathaniel always had an interest in Helena, but she rebuffed him at every turn... But that all happened a very long time ago."

"Before she was with Jacob Allwood?"

"I don't know if Helena was ever with Jacob. He certainly courted her, but I don't recall anything coming of it."

"Why didn't you tell me?"

"Are you asking me why I didn't divulge the details of your grandmother's love life?" Tessa countered. "For one, it's not my place to do so. Even if it was, why would I tell you about men that courted Helena long before you were born?"

"Maybe because these people are after me now," I snapped. I scrubbed my cheeks with my hands, and said, "Dan said that since witches are after me, maybe I should be careful around you."

"Dan sad that." The tea kettle whistled. Tessa got up and took the kettle off the burner, then she started slamming mugs onto the counter.

"Dan gave you an opinion on witches, and you listened to him," Tessa said with her back to me. "Up until a short time ago you ran from his sight, and now you trust his opinion on witches? On me?"

"Dan just said that maybe I should be careful around you." Tessa faced me, her arms crossed over her stomach and her face a mask of hurt. I'd just hurt my best friend.

"Tess, I am freaking out," I said, my voice catching as tears flowed down my cheeks. "I don't know what to do, but there are people—powerful people—after me, they've been after me a long time, and I don't want to get taken again." I flashed back to my captors choking me in that basement prison, and lost my breath. Dark spots hovered at the edge of my vision, and I felt consciousness slipping away... Then Tessa's cool hands were on my forehead and neck, and her soothing voice brought me out of the memory.

"Come back to me," she said. "Eliza, it's over. They can't hurt you anymore."

I gulped a lungful of air, humiliated and angry and so goddamned happy I could breathe. I slumped forward onto Tessa, and let her comfort me.

"I don't know what to do," I said around my sobs. "I'm freaking out. I don't think I can do this."

"Of course you can do this," Tessa said as she stroked my hair. "You have proven, time and again, that you can do anything."

"I don't want to do anything," I wailed. "I just want to be left alone."

"I wish I could make that happen for you." Tessa tightened her arms around me. "Our only option is to stop them, so they can't hurt you ever again."

Chapter 18

Trust Your Instincts

The next morning, my alarm went off, and I went for my run. Dan didn't call while I was out, and I finished my usual route in record time. My witchfinder, which I'd kept in my hand the entire time, didn't even heat up.

When I got back to my apartment, I stared at my phone, verifying and re-verifying that I hadn't missed any calls. Not that I was only checking for Dan's calls. Tessa hadn't called either, nor had Bennet, or anyone else I knew. It was as if the world spun on without me.

I should call Dan, check in on the case. My finger hovered over the call button for a moment, then I put the phone down. I was the one who complained that Dan called me too much, then at the first hint of silence from him I decided to call him? That was crazy talk. He had a life, and a full-time job, and probably a hundred things to do that were more important than calling me. I needed to get a grip and stop relying on Dan to fix all my problems.

That I'd come to rely on him in the first place was more than a bit disconcerting. As Tessa pointed out the day before, not that long ago, I ran from Dan's sight. Now I couldn't imagine passing an entire morning without talking to him, and that wasn't right. It wasn't fair to Dan, or to me.

Since I had no immediate way to counteract my newfound neediness, and I really didn't want to deal with reality, I took a shower.

Afterward, I went back out to the kitchen and found my apartment was still empty. I checked my phone; no missed calls.

My paranoid brain told me that now Tessa was avoiding me, too. The small, rational portion of my mind thought to check my appointment book, which was empty for the day. Tessa usually didn't come by in the morning if we didn't have any clients scheduled, since she liked to sleep late. At least, I hoped that's all it was.

I remembered how hurt she'd been yesterday, when I all but accused her of conspiring against me. Tessa would never hurt me, I knew that as surely as I knew my own name. What's more, if she'd actually been in on a plot to hand me over to Nathaniel Beauclaire, she could have done so hundreds if not thousands of times over the past eleven years. Instead, she'd been nothing but my friend, and I'd thrown that in her face.

Tessa claimed she understood, and that there were no hard feelings between us. Even so, I knew how sensitive she was. She had a big, gentle heart, and despite her great age, she'd never developed a thick skin. It was one of the reasons she was so easy to get along with. Tessa understood love and loss, and felt both deeply.

Maybe Tessa needs time apart from me. Like a century.

My phone buzzed, and I almost jumped out of my skin. I saw the local area code and assumed Dan was calling from the station. I accepted the call with an exuberant, "Good morning!"

"Good morning to you, too. I trust you slept well?"

I blinked; that Brahmin accent didn't belong to Dan, but I knew one adorable blond who loved playing British. "Hey, Nick. What can I do for you?"

"Actually, I was hoping to do something for you. Would you care to have lunch with me today? If you have time, of course. I know you're quite busy."

I stared out at my empty waiting room. "I have plenty of time. Where would you like to go?"

"I will text you the restaurant's address. Shall we meet at noon?"

I glanced at the clock. It was just after eleven. "We shall. See you then."

We ended the call, then I set my phone down and smiled. I didn't need Dan or Tessa to keep me company. I had a lunch date with a cute boy, and I was going to enjoy it. Today was working out to be just great.

***

It took me about thirty minutes to get to the restaurant. I stood next to the hostess station for a moment, then I saw Nick waving at me from one of the booths.

"Hey," I said as I slid into the booth across from him. "Thanks for inviting me."

"Thank you for accepting." He signaled to the server. A moment later, they brought me a menu and a glass of water.

"Have you ever eaten here before?" Nick asked.

"I've been here a few times." I scanned the lunch menu; sandwiches, sandwiches, and more sandwiches. All great options unless you were like me, and disliked sandwiches. As I contemplated the soup of the day—lentil, yum—my phone vibrated.

"Excuse me," I said as checked my phone; it was only a weather update. I slid it back into my pocket. As I did so, my knuckles brushed my witchfinder.

It was hot.

I froze, desperately trying not to freak out like I had during my run the day before. I was in a crowded restaurant, and there were at least four witch clans in the area. The odds of a witch or three having lunch in the restaurant I was in were pretty good. There was no reason to think the witch in question even knew who I was.

My phone buzzed again. "Sorry," I said, grateful for the distraction. "It's probably work."

"Please," Nick said, indicating my phone.

That notification was an email response from my dad about my protection tattoo. According to him, the tattoo would flare if it was touched by a witch.

My witchfinder was hot. Nick had made my witch-sensitive tattoo flare. But, Nick wasn't a witch.

Was he?

"Are you all right?" Nick asked. "You've gone rather pale."

"What? Yes," I replied. "Just thinking about something from work. Sorry."

"Have you taken on any new and interesting cases?"

"Oh, always." I turned my attention back to the menu as my heart hammered against my ribs. "Never a dull moment at Nine Lives Investigations."

"Wherever did you come up with that name?"

"Oh, it's all because of my gran. She has these three cats that have stuck around practically forever." I flipped the menu over, and kept reading instead of meeting Nick's gaze while simultaneously pretending I could actually stomach food in light of what was happening. "We call them the Feline Federation. Anyway, I named the business after the old saying about cats having nine lives."

"Are you close with your... gran, did you say?"

"Yeah. I grew up with her."

"Do you miss her?"

I lowered the menu. "I never said she was gone."

"Forgive me, I assumed."

"Sure. No problem."

Movement near the entrance caught my eye; Tessa was standing there. Relief flooded me. My witchfinder hadn't been alerting me to Tessa—since she made it, she was immune—but If Tessa was with me it wouldn't matter. She was more than capable of sussing out and dealing with any type of threat, witch or otherwise.

"My friend's waiting for a table," I said. "Would you mind if she joined us?"

Nick smiled. "Not at all. I'm sure all of us sitting together will be great fun."

I grinned, then I waved my arm until I got Tessa's attention. She hesitated before she approached our table.

"This place is packed," I said when she was close enough. "Want to sit with us?"

"And who is us?" Tessa asked. Nick looked up and smiled. Tessa went white as a sheet.

"You," Tessa said, taking a step back. "Get away from Eliza, now!"

"You two know each other?" I asked. "Tess, what's wrong?" When she didn't answer, I said, "I didn't realize you'd met Nick."

"Nick?" she repeated. "Is that what you're calling yourself these days?"

"What would you prefer?" Nick asked.

Tessa ignored him. "Eliza, get behind me."

"Eliza, do not move," Nick said. I tried to get up. I couldn't move a finger.

"Release her, Nathaniel," Tessa demanded. "This is a public place, and you know I don't care for messes. You will release Eliza, now, and you will deal with me."

"Will I, Tessie? And what will you do? There aren't any more seers to protect you from me."

"I don't need anyone's protection." Tessa clenched her fist, and I saw depressions on the sides of Nick's throat in the shape of fingers. "Eliza, now."

I slid out of the booth, and Tessa took my seat. "What's going on?"

"This beast is Nathaniel Beauclaire," Tessa replied. "He's the sort of witch that ruined our reputation with the mortals a long, long time ago." Tessa glanced at me. "If he brought you here, he's trying to distract you."

"Cecily," I said. "It's her, isn't it?"

"Trust your instincts," Tessa said, then she tightened her grip on Nathaniel. His eyes bulged, proof of his constricted airway. "Go. Deal with Cecily. I can handle Nathaniel."

"Thanks, Tess. I owe you."

Tessa laughed. "The pleasure is all mine."

I went out the back door of the restaurant and stood on the patio. It was still too early in the season for it to be in use, so I stood among the empty tables and gathered my thoughts. Nick Allwood was actually Nathaniel Beauclaire, which meant Jada probably wasn't his sister. She was probably some random kid he and his crazy dead mother-in-law had been holding hostage for decades.

I needed to find Jada, get her out from under Nathaniel's influence and get her some real help. Were her parents still alive, wondering what had happened to their daughter? Did they even remember having a daughter?

I needed to talk to Dan.

I pulled out my phone and called his work phone, but it went straight to voice mail. I called his personal cell, then his home number. Same. Finally, I called the station back and asked for forensics.

"Detective Lyons didn't come in today," Jill said. After a pause, she added, "Unscheduled."

"Thanks." I slid my phone into my pocket, then I started running to my car. Dan was the most reliable man on earth. If he hadn't come into work it was because he had been purposefully kept from going there, and I could only think of one person who felt threatened by my mortal partner.

Cecily Allwood.

Chapter 19

Everyone Knew Helena

Think, think, think.

If they took Dan, they must have brought him somewhere secure. The most secure place Cecily had access to was the Allwood Compound.

I was not equipped to go up against the Allwood clan. Hell, I wasn't equipped to go up against a single irritated witch without some serious, Tessa-sized backup. But the Allwoods had Dan, I was certain of it. If it hadn't been for me, Dan would have gone through life without knowing the supernatural was real. The Allwoods had only taken him because of me.

I was going to get Dan back, no matter what.

I got in my car and saw the cookbook lying on the dashboard. Tessa had said the recipes were lists of assets, while the pictures of food had been hiding maps of important locations. What if Dan was at one of these locations? I'd flipped through the book, but I couldn't figure out what locations these maps represented. I needed someone who could understand and explain this book to me, fast.

I started driving toward the eastern side of town. I'd never been inside the Allwood Compound, but I knew where it was; on a hill that overlooked most of the town. My gran's house was at the base of the hill. She'd always stood between the witches and the mortals, much as all seers stood between life and death. We were the bridges between worlds, the safe haven for supernatural and mortal alike, those who were still alive and those who had already passed on. We were the walls that kept everyone safe.

Cecily had violated one of the oldest rules of our community: supernaturals are to leave mortals be. Up until about a year ago, it would have been Gran's job to set things right. As of today, that job is mine.

All of this newfound resolve increased my chances of rescuing Dan exactly zero percent, and I didn't have a backup plan. Or an initial plan, for that matter. If I'd had time, I could have gone to Gran's, researched her books and notes, and come up with a way to decimate the Allwoods. I could have contacted Bennet, and he could have contacted other shepherds to assist me. I could have called Tessa, but she was guarding Nathaniel Beauclaire; he was our biggest problem, but not the most pressing. Still, seers were meant to work with witches, and I knew just where to find one that would definitely be on my side.

I altered my course and turned onto Suffolk Street. A ghost's presence is always strongest where they died. Since Jacob Allwood's body had expired on this street, it was where I was hoping to catch his spirit.

I pulled into the driveway at number fifty-four, cut the engine, and thought. Yellow police tape was wrapped around the front porch, and one of those push button combination locks real estate agents used was securing the door. I probably could have picked the back door's lock or even broken a window, but I didn't have the time or the energy for that. Instead, I went old school.

"Jacob Allwood," I yelled. "Jacob Allwood, I am summoning your dead ass to me this instant!"

"I'm here."

I looked in the rearview mirror, saw him staring at me from the back seat. "Up front."

A moment later, he was in the passenger seat. "I assume something quite dire has occurred for you to summon me in this manner."

"It appears that Cecily is Nathaniel Beauclaire's bitch."

"Ah, well." Jacob looked down at his hands, folded in his lap. "Cecily feels slighted by many things. She's much younger than me, and not nearly as—"

"Save the sob story. She's got a grudge, and she's kidnapped my partner. I need to get him back."

"She has the detective?"

"She does. You can tell me all about why she has a grudge against my family after Dan's safe. For now, I need you to help me get inside your house, and get him out."

"Why should I go against my own clan for you?"

"Two reasons. One, I think your own clan already went against you. How could Cecily have no idea how your body left the compound and ended up here, dead?"

Jacob's gaze flitted to the house, then it returned to me. "I have wondered that, myself."

"And who trapped you at the orchard? Who could have trapped you? Maybe, Nathaniel Beauclaire?"

Jacob's eyes flashed. "That man is an abomination."

"Agreed. Tessa's keeping an eye on him."

"Finally, a bit of good news." Jacob regarded me. "Your reasons are sound."

"All of that was only the first reason. As for the second, you are well aware that my gran was the matriarch of seers. As of today, that position is filled by me."

Jacob nodded approvingly. "Brava, Miss Moore. Helena would be proud."

"Helena would be pissed. Cecily broke rules, and Gran would have taught her a lesson the clan would never forget." I paused, the pieces finally falling into place. I understood how I could save Dan, punish Cecily, and keep anything like what happened to Jada Allwood from happening ever again.

As of today, I step into Gran's shoes. I am the matriarch.

"Help me today, and any punishments will be Cecily's alone," I said to Jacob. "The rest of your clan won't suffer for her crimes."

"That is an admirable offer," Jacob said. "But what of Beauclaire?"

"Stay on with me, and we can take him down together."

***

The thing with houses on a hill was not only the excellent view you got from within the house in all directions, you also saw it long before you got to it. The twenty-minute drive to the Allwood Compound seemed to take twenty years, while the creepy old manor loomed over us the entire time.

"When did Sarah Allwood die?" I asked, when the silence became unbearable.

"Oh, long ago. Long, long ago." Jacob studied the compact houses as we passed them. I wondered if this was the longest he'd ever spent in a neighborhood with such a low tax bracket. "All of this, this mess we're attempting to clean up. It's not entirely Nathaniel's fault."

"How's that?"

"He was one of Sarah's victims. We all were, at one time or another. She was an evil woman, and unfortunately her cruelty was only matched by her natural ability with magic."

"Is that why her daughter married Beauclaire? To get away from her mother?"

"Jemima and Nathaniel loved each other. They always have. But when Nathaniel learned how Sarah treated not only Jemima, but all of her children..."

Jacob shook his head. "Nathaniel thought that by killing Sarah he would save his wife, and the rest of the clan. He only did it out of love for Jemima."

"He murdered his wife's mother out of love?"

Jacob met my gaze. "It was his best option. The whole of the clan supported him, but we'd lived too long without a seer to understand what we were doing. I was so young I'd never even met a seer. We were isolated here in the New World, you see."

"What went wrong?"

"Nathaniel assumed that if there were no fresh corpses present when Sarah died her spirit would be forced to move on."

"But Sarah was too strong," I surmised. "Therefore, Nathaniel not only killed her, he got to be tormented by her ghost." I glanced at Jacob. "What did she do to him?"

"It's not what she did, so much as what she showed him. The fact that she lives on, even now, made Nathaniel realize that for all his power, there were untold worlds he had yet to experience, let alone conquer. He wishes to straddle life and death, and exert control over both."

"But witches don't do that," I began, then I fell silent. Seers could control life and death.

"Do you know how he knew my gran?"

"Firstly, everyone knew Helena," Jacob said, his voice warming when he said Gran's name. "She was a quiet woman, but only a fool mistook her quietness for weakness. Helena was confident in her strength, had no reason to brag."

"You loved her."

"I did."

"Did she love you?"

"I... I like to think she did. However, that was the problem. That is the problem, still. Long ago, Nathaniel courted Helena. At first he was only interested in her as a seer, but he was soon captivated by her. The feeling was not mutual."

"I bet. Gran had excellent taste in men. How did Beauclaire take to you hanging around with Gran?"

"For the longest time, he didn't know. He'd returned to Europe, and truth be told I never met Helena until after he'd gone. I was as captivated by her as he'd been."

"This was after Adesh died?" I asked. Adesh was my grandfather. He'd passed when my father was still young.

"Yes. Adesh had been gone for four or five years."

I bit the inside of my mouth to keep from asking more questions about Jacob's relationship with my grandmother. Some things were better left unsaid.

"When Beauclaire came back and found you and Gran hanging around, he must have been pretty irritated."

"Yes. Yes, he was. But then you were born, and he hatched a new plan."

I turned the last corner, and we reached the Allwood compound's massive gates. "This place is a fortress," I said, leaning toward the windshield to get a better view of the very high walls.

"Nigh on impregnable."

I grabbed the cookbook from between the seats and set it on the dash. "This book is filled with maps. Can it help us get inside?"

"Where did you find this?" Jacob asked. "And I can grant us access. This is still my house. I will simply tell them to let us in." He looked down at himself, frowned. "Gods, I forgot they can't see me."

A guard approached us. I pushed up my sleeve and reached toward Jacob. "Make contact with me," I said.

Jacob touched my arm. I closed my eyes and fed him enough energy to make him appear solid. When the guard rapped on my window, I rolled it down, but it was Jacob who spoke.

"Hello, Sims. Open the gate."

"M-Mr. Allwood, I'd heard—"

"What you heard was my request that you open my gate. Shall I make it an order?"

"No, sir. Right away."

Sims, smart person that he was, returned to the guard shack and punched in a code. The gate creaked open, and we drove on through.

"Where to?" I asked.

"Take the road on the left. We can leave the car with the staff vehicles, and enter through the kitchen."

I drove down the curved road and found the parking area Based on the amount of cars already present the Allwoods employed a lot of people. "What happened to Jemima?"

"Jemima. Poor, sweet, naïve Jemima." Jacob studied his fingernails for a moment. "I've been a spirit for so long I'd forgotten I had fingernails. I was losing all sense of my body, but I never realized it until you made me a bit more corporeal. Were you aware that spirits lose themselves in such a way?"

"Yeah. I was."

"Yes, well, I'm sure that Helena taught you well." Jacob pulled the cookbook onto his lap and thumbed through it. "About Jemima, she never really had a sense of herself. She'd come of age under the long shadow of her mother, Sarah, and then she was swept up in her love for Nathaniel. When she fell ill, and Sarah told Nathaniel how to keep Jemima with him for all eternity, both believed her."

I parked the car. "Jemima died before Sarah?"

"Oh, no. Sarah had been dead for years, but her spirit never moved on. It was her resilience that gave Nathaniel the notion he could somehow cheat death." Jacob smiled, but it didn't reach his eyes. "No one can cheat death, you know."

"I believe you."

"Be careful who you believe, Miss Moore. Jemima and Nathaniel believed Sarah, when she told them that they should let Jemima's body die so her spirit could soar. Sarah assured them that she would tether Jemima to herself and this world."

When Jacob fell silent, I said, "But that didn't happen."

"It did not. Jemima's spirit was captured by Sarah, and for all this time she's been holding her trapped between planes. Could you imagine making your own daughter suffer so?"

"That's awful," I said. "But why would Sarah do such a thing? Revenge for her murder?"

"Perhaps. Or perhaps it's more of her own twisted nature revealing itself. Regardless, Sarah has held the promise of a reunion with Jemima over Nathaniel's head ever since. It's how she's gotten him to do whatever she says, which is why he was so pleased when you were born."

"How did my birth affect his plans?"

"Sarah's longtime goal has been to possess a powerful seer. Nathaniel monitored your life, and arranged for her to possess you when you were still a child. Unfortunately, she possessed a different girl."

I swallowed the lump in my throat. "But, Nathaniel went along with my plan to exorcise Sarah from Jada."

"Yes, I imagine he did, because that's also part of the plan. Once Sarah is in your body, she will return Jemima to Nathaniel—then

Nathaniel will do away with Sarah altogether and install Jemima in you."

I closed my eyes and slowed my breathing, concentrating on the feel of the steering wheel beneath my hands. "Is that what he tried doing then I was seventeen?"

"Yes."

The full realization of what Jacob was telling me numbed me, body and soul. Nathaniel hadn't just wanted a seer. He'd wanted a glorified sex doll. Gran had evaded him, and he laid low until he tried the same plan with me. One thing he'd forgotten, us Moore girls don't go down without a fight.

Usually, we don't go down at all.

"Miss Moore, I assure you that the bulk of my clan—oh, bloody hell."

I cracked an eyelid, and saw that Jacob had tried patting my arm but had gotten frustrated when his ethereal form passed right through me. Somehow, that small act of kindness only increased my resolve. The Allwoods as a whole were good people. Nathaniel and Cecily were not, and I would deal with them accordingly.

"It's the thought that counts," I said, and the ghost smiled at me. "And call me Eli. All my friends do."

"Very well, Eli." Jacob mustered a bit of solidity, and showed me one of the maps in the book. "This book lists the Allwood assets, and this is a map of the estate. If the detective is here, he will be in the wine cellar. Make note of the cellar's layout, and what it's next to."

I glanced at the map, then the house in front of us. To the west of the kitchen was what looked like a burial ground. "Are those your ancestors?"

"They are. Don't worry, Sarah's not among them."

"Good to know." I took another look at the map, then I got out of the car the old-fashioned way while Jacob floated through the door. "Let's get my partner back, then we can work on cleaning up the rest of your sister's mess."

CHAPTER 20

A CIRCLE UNBROKEN

Getting inside the main house was easy. According to Jacob, the side door to the kitchen was normally left unlocked during the day to receive deliveries. We simply walked in, then ducked into the pantry to discuss our next move.

"Which way to the wine cellar?" I asked.

Jacob indicated a hallway. "It will be the third door on the left. While you see to him, I will visit Cecily and see what I can learn about her plans."

"All right," I said. "If you feel weak, come find me. I'll give you a boost."

"Thank you, Eli."

With that, my new ghost buddy dissipated. I hoped he knew what he was doing, and that he could hold his own against his psycho sister. The question remained, exactly what did Cecily stand to gain from all this?

Worry about that later. I checked the hallway. It was empty, so I headed to the wine cellar door. Locked. As I knelt and withdrew my lock picks, I wondered if they always kept this door locked, or if they only did when they had prisoners on site. Based on the lame doorknob lock they used to secure the cellar, I was betting on the latter.

Lock dealt with, I eased the door open and closed it behind me, and waited for my eyes to adjust to the low light. As the room came into focus, I realized this wasn't just a wine cellar. From the unusually ornate wooden staircase to the rows and rows of cabinets shoved against the walls, it was an exact match for the room I'd been held in eleven years ago.

I crept down the stairs, shocked and terrified and hardly believing my eyes. The steps descended to a packed dirt floor, which some would find odd at the bottom of a staircase as ostentatious as this one. I understood that for certain rituals, direct contact with the earth was ideal. To my left was a wall of metal lockers, most of which were closed. The single open locker held stacks of folded cloth in the bottom portion, while the upper shelf was packed with dried herbs and cork-topped bottles.

To my right, the room opened up in a way I hadn't been able to see from the steps, and it was further divided with black sheets that were hung from the ceiling beams. My captors had done that to me, too, to further isolate and disorient me. It had worked.

I worked my way through the maze of sheets, barely keeping my panic at bay. When I'd been abducted, my last act of defiance had been to rip down the sheets and set them on fire with a lighter I'd scavenged from a dark, forgotten corner. I'd hoped to set the whole house ablaze and get the fire department to come out. I probably would have died, too, but at the time I was pretty sure they were going to kill me anyway, and if I was going to die I wanted to take as many of my captors with me as I could. Now that I knew how Nathaniel wanted me to permanently house his dead wife's spirit, death would have been preferable. I stepped around another sheet, and found Dan sprawled across the dirt floor.

"Hey, buddy." I dropped to my knees and felt his neck, searching for a pulse. He was cold as a corpse and wasn't moving, and the ground around him was wet. I remembered my captors dousing me with buckets of water; when I'd complained about my cold, wet clothes, they'd taken them. If only that had been the worst thing that happened to me in that basement. Dan was still wearing his clothes, except for his shoes, but everything was soaked.

"There it is," I said, having located his pulse. "Let's get this mess off of you."

I rolled him flat onto his back and unbuttoned his shirt. Once I'd gotten that top layer off him I pulled his tee shirt up and over his head, then I peeled off his socks. I had no idea where his shoes had gotten to, and his pants could stay right where they were. That done, I took off my leather jacket, leaned against the cellar wall and positioned Dan so his upper body was against mine, and draped my jacket over him like a blanket.

"Come on," I said, as I rubbed heat into his arms. "I need you to wake up. I can't carry you out of here. You need to walk. You need to come back to me, and we will walk out of here together."

Dan twitched, the second proof of life he'd given me, but that was it. I pressed my cheek against the top of his head, trying to transfer energy into him the way I did with spirits. I dug deep, pulling on energy reserves I hadn't realized were there.

"I can't do this without you," I said, hating the desperation in my voice, hating Cecily for hurting Dan and making me desperate in the first place. "Dan, please."

He twitched again, then his arm snaked around my waist. "That's it," I said, relief pouring into my voice as tears flowed down my face. "Keep moving. You're going to be okay."

"Eli?" Dan's voice was a warm rumble against my chest. "What happened?"

"Witches kidnapped you. I'm going to get you out of here."

"I'm feeling...something. Is this you?"

"I'm feeding you energy."

I felt Dan's face, which was pressed against my neck, stretch into a smile. "I guess you do like me."

I sank my fingers into his damp hair. "Yeah. I like you."

Jacob picked that moment to appear in front of us. "You found him," Jacob began, then he tilted his head to the side as he regarded us. "Fascinating."

"What's fascinating?" I asked.

"Huh?" Dan asked.

"Jacob's here." I pushed up my sleeve, and pressed my seer's mark against Dan's bare back. "There. You'll be able to hear and see him now." I looked up at Jacob, and asked, "What's fascinating?"

"I can see the energy flowing between you." Eyes wide, Jacob leaned closer to us. "Not only are you feeding him energy, he is reciprocating. You two are quite the pair." Jacob rubbed his chin. "A circle unbroken."

I did not have the spoons to deal with Jacob's assessment of Dan and me, so I set it aside. "Did you learn anything from Cecily?"

"Yes. Apparently, all of this is a trap."

All at once the black fabric maze fell to the ground, revealing Cecily and a dozen others surrounding us. "You could have led with that," I hissed at Jacob.

"Aren't you two sweet," Cecily said. "I knew you were unnaturally attached to this mortal. Sickening."

Something's off. I glanced at Jacob. "Cecily doesn't know I'm here," he said. "I thought it best not to reveal myself."

"Good plan," I said. Cecily smiled, since she thought I was talking about her.

"Why, thank you," she said. "Going forward I assume you'll approve of all my plans. From now on you're my seer. No one else will use your abilities but me."

"What about Detective Lyons?" I asked. "Will he be your personal police force?"

"He will be my insurance. As long as I have him, I'm sure you'll comply."

Cecily turned away to address her evil henchmen. Nothing like being underestimated by the bad guys. While I wracked my brain for a plan one of Dan's hands slid underneath my shirt and roamed across my back, while the other felt inside my waistband. "What are you doing?" I whispered.

"Looking for your weapons."

"Left side."

I drew my knee up so my calf was hidden underneath my jacket. Instead of going there to retrieve my self-defense baton, Dan lifted up my butt.

"Hey," I said, then he drew my phone out of my back pocket. Leaving him to whatever plan he had, I said to both Cecily and Jacob, "So, what's next?"

"Next?" Cecily turned back to me. "Next, you will ensure that Nathaniel Beauclaire leaves my clan be. Next, you will ensure that this ridiculous inquiry into Jacob's death is halted. Next, you will do whatever I require of you, immediately and without complaint."

"That's a lot of nexts," I said. "Also, I complain a lot."

Cecily's nostrils flared, always an elegant look. She gestured to one of her goons, who approached me with a baseball bat. Why would a witch carry a baseball bat?

"These aren't witches," I said. Cecily's eyes widened and she took a step back. "You've got mortals protecting you, not your clan!"

"Silence," Cecily said, but I've never been good at following orders.

"Your clan either doesn't know what you're doing, or they don't support you," I said. "Do they know what you did to Jacob?"

"Shut her up," Cecily ordered.

The goon raised his bat.

I glanced around for an escape route but we were against a wall, literally backed into a corner. I shrank down, steeling myself for the hit. "Incoming," I warned Dan.

Dan flung my jacket aside, jumped up, and punched the goon square in the face. He dropped like a stone as Dan similarly took out the two men behind him. I'd given Dan so much energy he became Super Dan.

"Who's next?" Dan said to the rest of Cecily's goons. "I've got a score to settle with all of you."

Dan can't fight everyone. "How does a seer stop a witch?" I asked Jacob.

"You can't, but you don't need to," Jacob said. "They can."

"Who is they?"

"We've been burying our dead at the compound for several centuries," Jacob explained. "They're all here, waiting. They—we—will help you." Jacob glanced at Dan, and said, "I daresay they're already helping."

"Waiting for what?" I demanded, then I realized.

I spoke to the dead.

All of that extra energy I'd funneled to Dan had come from the generations of Allwoods buried on the grounds. They didn't want Cecily to succeed.

They wanted to help me.

"Allwoods," I shrieked, because subtlety be damned. "Allwoods, Cecily is ruining your family name! Allwoods, I need your help!"

One by one, I felt the Allwoods of the past slip out of their graves and join me in the wine cellar. Soon the room was packed with dozens—no, hundreds—of spirits, all of them waiting to do my bidding.

Only, they didn't know me.

"Jacob," I said. "Tell them to stop Cecily."

He cracked his ethereal knuckles. "That, we shall do."

***

When Dan and I emerged from the basement, the compound was packed with police cruisers.

"I see you called 911 before you hulked out."

"I did." He handed me my phone. "I don't know what you did to me down there, but I feel fantastic."

"Wait until it wears off," I said. "From what I've been told these energy hangovers are no joke."

"Then I guess I'd best make the most of this one," Dan said, as he draped his arm around my shoulders.

"Yeah? Got something planned?"

"There is something I've been waiting a while for," he said, then he pulled me against him and kissed me hard.

I didn't pull away. I didn't even give his chest a halfhearted shove. As I wound my arms around his neck and kissed him back, I realized I'd been waiting for this, too.

The fireworks I'd felt when Nick—I mean Nathaniel—had kissed me? They were a burnt out match compared to what I felt with Dan.

When we parted he grinned at me, then Dan was whisked away by the first responders. As I watched Dan—shirtless, muscular, and hopped up on spirit energy—explain to the police what had happened, I thought about what Jacob said: we'd shared our energy with each other. "A circle unbroken". Just as I made a mental note to research that term, Tessa came running toward me.

"I'm so glad you're safe," she said, pulling me into her arms." "Eliza, I was terrified! Actually terrified!"

"So was I." I hugged her, so glad my Tessa was back. "I'm sorry things got weird between us."

"It's all right. Weirdness abounds in our lives." Tessa held me at arms length. "I'm so sorry, but I had to let Nathaniel go. He threatened to kill us along with everyone else in the restaurant, and I believed him."

"You did the right thing," I said. "Cecily was today's biggest evil. We can worry about the rest tomorrow."

Tessa draped her arm around my shoulders as my arm slid around her waist. "Why aren't any of these fine officers speaking to you?"

"I think they're all shocked and relieved Dan is safe." I know I was.

"My, he does look good without a shirt on."

"They took his shoes, too."

"Eliza Jayne, if you're more concerned with the soles of Dan's feet than those godlike biceps, I officially call dibs on that man."

"Go ahead. He likes you."

Dan glanced over his shoulder and smiled at me. I smiled back. Unfortunately, Tessa saw the whole thing.

"Believe me," she said, "I do not stand a chance with him."

CHAPTER 21

PARTNERS?

It didn't take long for the police to sort things out at the Allwood Compound. The official story was that Cecily Allwood, in a bid to take control of the family's considerable wealth, had murdered her older brother and had his body dumped at the Suffolk Street residence. After being questioned by the police, Cecily got nervous and had the investigating officer, Dan, kidnapped to shut him up. The official report conveniently overlooked a lot of things, but Cecily was in jail and the rest of her clan was safe, and that was what mattered.

Something else that mattered was Jada. Tessa warded the hospital where Jada was an inpatient, which made it impossible for Nathaniel Beauclaire to enter. Since he wasn't really Jada's brother, our next priority became tracking down her real family. Since I was the resident private investigator, that job was mine.

I was happy to do the legwork. After all Jada had endured, reuniting her with her family was the least I could do.

As for Dan, he crashed hard after the spirit energy wore off. He slept for sixteen solid hours, and said he could probably sleep for sixteen more. I did not envy him.

Three days after Cecily had been locked up, Tessa, Bennet, Jacob, and I had breakfast at my place. The energy I'd pumped into Jacob seemed to settle into him, and he was solid enough to be seen and heard by everyone, not just seers. We all wondered how long it would last. Sarah Allwood's creepy cookbook was in the center of the table, and for Bennet that was as good as a present on Christmas morning.

"Helena had this in her solarium?" Bennet asked, as he paged through the book for the third time. "Fascinating."

"Helena regularly brought out one surprise, only to follow it with another," Jacob said.

"She was always up to something," Tessa said. "Mischief was her middle name."

"Gran, mischievous?" I said. I loved hearing these old stories about her. It kept her memory close, which was just where I wanted it. "She kept that side hidden away when I was around."

"You should have seen here when she was young," Tessa and Jacob said in concert, then we all laughed.

"Anyone want more coffee?" I asked, then I realized the sugar bowl was empty. I hopped up onto the counter so I could get the box of sugar from the upper shelf. I was still sitting on the counter when Dan peeked in through the back door.

"Okay if I come in?" he asked.

"Definitely," I replied. We hadn't seen each other in days, and I'd missed him. Before I could say hello or ask him how he was, I realized that Tessa, Bennet, and even Jacob were watching us.

"Tess," I hissed.

"What? Oh, yes. Bennet, Jacob, come with me into the waiting room." Tessa stood as the other two followed suit.

"What's in the waiting room?" Bennet asked.

"You'll see," Tessa said. Then they were gone, and Dan and I were alone in the kitchen.

"Tessa really is the one in charge," Dan said.

"She is the oldest," I said. "How's your spiritual energy hangover?"

"There is not enough aspirin in the world to make me want to try that again. But, it was fun being super strong for a while." He leaned his elbow on the counter next to my hip. "I don't know how I can ever thank you."

"You don't have to. You said you always have my back, and now you know I've got yours."

"Yeah. I do." He moved closer, and laid his arm on the counter behind my hips. "Sorry if I got a little handsy with you in the basement, and afterward."

"It's okay." I draped my arms over his shoulders. "We can blame it on the near-death experience."

"So." Dan's lazy, half-lidded gaze was making my stomach do somersaults. "What are we now?"

"We aren't still Dan and Eli?"

"I think we're a little beyond that."

"Partners, then?" I ruffled the hair above the nape of his neck. He'd let it grow out a bit, and it was starting to curl. I liked that. "Although you got shot down when you tried to make me a police consultant."

"Maybe I can be your consultant. Help you out when things get weird." He paused, then asked, "Around here, things get weird, often, don't they?"

"They do." My fingers moved from his hair down to his neck. He was deliciously warm, and my perpetually cold fingers drank in the heat. "Jacob called us a circle unbroken."

"I remember. What's that mean?"

"Honestly, I have no idea."

The corner of his mouth curled up. "We can figure it out together. Maybe you'll finally let me take you to lunch."

"We're still just coworkers," I said. "All of that at the Allwood house was a one-off."

"What do I have to do to get promoted to more than coworker?" he asked, and I smiled. "Wait, I know. I need to crack the next case."

"That's a start. We should probably begin with Nick Allwood."

"That kid again?"

"Oh, I forgot to tell you. Jada's not his sister, and he's actually Nathaniel Beauclaire."

Dan took a step back. "What?"

***

Is this your first time meeting Eli, Dan, and Tessa? Pick up the free prequel, Belladonna, available on my Patreon page, and here: https:/ /dl.bookfunnel.com/bsixnoflia

The story continues in Bleeding Hearts, Poison Garden #2 Keep scrolling for a sneak peek!

Bleeding Hearts

Chapter One

I read the business's street number, then I checked it against the scrap of paper in my hand. "This is it?"

"According to my divination spell, yes." Tessa tossed her bouncy, shiny hair behind her shoulder, the dark strands reflecting like polished onyx in the early morning light. She was like a living, breathing shampoo commercial. "What's so unusual about it?"

"For starters, it's a Chinese restaurant, and Nathaniel Beauclaire's a witch who was born in tenth century England."

Tessa shrugged, sending all those perfectly loose waves cascading over her shoulder once again. She was like Medusa, but shiny. "Hiding out in a foreign culture's neighborhood is a common tactic that has been used by those on the run since time immemorial."

"I don't know if one restaurant constitutes a neighborhood." This city didn't have a Chinatown, or any other cultural hubs to speak of. The city council liked to refer to themselves as diverse and inclusive, but once you got past the four blocks that comprised the downtown area it was upper middle class Caucasians as far as the eye could see.

"And doesn't Nathaniel prefer expensive places?" I added. "I can't see him hanging out near an all you can eat lunch buffet."

"Hence the 'hiding out' aspect, as I said earlier." Tessa leaned closer to the window, shielding her eyes as she scoped out the interior. "I don't see anyone, and the lights are off. Let's go inside."

I frowned, then I knelt in front of the door and got to work picking the lock. Tessa could have unlocked the door in a hot second with her witchcraft, but if Nathaniel really was inside the use of magic might alert him. We'd been tracking him for too long, and had experienced too many close calls, to make a rookie mistake now.

In addition to Nathaniel Beauclaire, we were also on the lookout for his murderous mother-in-law, Sarah Allwood. She'd died several hundred years ago, but her incredibly powerful spirit had hung around to make life miserable for her descendants. Most recently, she'd possessed a childhood friend of mine, Jada, for the past twenty years.

Sarah had been attempting to possess me, all with the ultimate goal of merging her considerably strong witchcraft with my seer abilities. As much as I wish Jada had never been possessed at all, I was so, so grateful I'd dodged that bullet.

It didn't take me long to disengage the lock. It hadn't been a very challenging lock, which was the latest disappointment in our frustrating pursuit of Nathaniel. Ever since Nathaniel had been revealed as Cecily Allwood's co-conspirator in the death of her brother, Jacob, Tess and I had been tracking Nathaniel with the intent of stopping him once and for all. For Tessa, that meant sending him off this mortal coil to finally be with his much loved and already deceased wife, Jemima. I wasn't down with such a final solution, and was hoping to incapacitate him with a binding spell instead. Tessa had agreed to consider the binding spell and other non-lethal options, but she hadn't made any promises.

I pushed open the restaurant's door. It went as easily as the lock had. "This is not a secure location," I observed.

"Is it still in business?" Tessa entered the dark restaurant and stood next to the hostess station. She ran a finger over the shiny wood menu stand. "Not a speck of dust."

"Weird." I stepped behind the bar, which was stocked for the lunch rush right down to the full ice bin. "The ice hasn't even melted. Where's the bartender, and the cooks? The waitresses?"

"And, where are all the customers," Tess added. She pulled a piece of spelled paper out of her back pocket and flung it into the air. I hung immobile for a moment, then it disintegrated into a cloud of rainbow-hued dust. "We're not under a stasis spell. So where is everyone?"

"Could Nathaniel have made everyone invisible?"

Tessa gave me a look. "It's easier to kill someone and trap their spirit than to cast a proper invisibility spell."

Before I could ask how the hell she knew that, my phone chirped. "Goddammit," I hissed.

"Turn that off," Tessa said. "You'll alert Nathaniel."

"As if he can't hear us talking. If he's even here." I withdrew my phone and glanced at the screen. It was a text from Dan.

Dan: You free?
Eli: I'm breaking into a Chinese restaurant. You?
Dan: I am going to assume that's a joke.

"Making a date?" Tessa looked over my shoulder. "Oh, tell Dan I said hello."

"You are so nosy."

Eli: Tess says hi. What's up?
Dan: Hey, Tessa

Dan: The new track at the college is complete. Want to go for a run?

"You should go," Tessa said. "It's been months since you two had your moment. You need to rekindle that spark."

"There is no spark," I muttered. "At least, there shouldn't be."

Before I could fire off a response to Dan, I felt a familiar tingle on the back of my neck. "There's a spirit nearby," I said.

"Let's hope they're friendly," Tessa murmured.

I cleared my throat, and said, "You can come closer. We won't hurt you."

Nothing happened, and no one materialized. "You're certain one is nearby?" Tessa asked.

"Yeah." I came out from behind the bar, and followed the sensation into the kitchen. "It's stronger in here."

Tessa entered the kitchen, and leaned against the salad station. Like everything else, the day's ingredients had been prepped and were waiting to be assembled. "Maybe it's a former owner, or someone who worked here?" she asked, as she swiped a slice of cucumber. "Vegetables are fresh."

"Yeah. Maybe it's a cook." What was extremely strange was that I felt the spirit, but they hadn't come forward when I spoke to them. Some ghosts hung around places for years waiting for someone to notice them. Here I was, ready to interact, and they were hiding from me. Why would they do that?

What if someone had told them to hide?

"Tess, I think we should get out of here."

"Why?" she asked, and I heard something click behind me. I turned around. The clicks had come from the stove.

My phone chirped; it was another text from Dan.

Dan: Run. Yes or No?
Eli: One sec.

As I watched, the knobs on the stove turned to the on position. Then the gas ignited and flames shot toward the ceiling.

"Get down," I shrieked as I dove under the worktable. I couldn't see Tessa but I heard metal clattering, like hail on a tin roof. I stuck my hand out but snatched it back when something metallic hit me. Knives bounced off the stainless steel worktable and hit the floor around me like the world's deadliest rainfall.

And, they kept falling. Dozens of knives—all of them wickedly sharp cooking blades—rained down from the ceiling, so many knives they piled up in the corners like snowdrifts.

"Why does this place have so much cutlery," I yelled.

"I don't think they're real," Tessa yelled back, then the clattering stopped. I waited for a moment, then I got out from under the table. Tessa was right. The knives were gone.

"Tess," I called. "Tessa, are you okay?"

"I'm fine." I heard movement near the salad station. Tessa stood up and brushed lettuce leaves and shredded carrots off her arms. "I'm covered in vegetables, but otherwise unharmed."

"I guess Nathaniel really was here." Something on the counter caught my eye; it was an old-fashioned

metal buckle, the kind grade schoolers wore on Pilgrim hats in school plays. "Why is this here?"

"Why is what here?" Tessa asked, then stopped short when she saw the buckle. "Oh."

"Oh, what?"

"Nathaniel's surname, Beauclaire, is derived from *bouclier*. It means buckle maker."

I picked up the buckle. "I guess that makes this evidence."

My phone chirped. I picked up my phone—luckily, the screen hadn't shattered—and saw that Dan had texted again. "Are we done here?"

Tessa plucked a radish out of her hair. "Oh, we're done all right."

Eli: I could use a run. Meet you there in an hour?
Dan: Sounds like a plan.

I slid my phone in my pocket and turned to Tessa. "Getting attacked with knives is a new and awful thing."

"At least they weren't real," she replied. "Where's our ghost?"

"Gone." I looked at the stove, and the knobs that had turned on the gas. With enough energy, a ghost could definitely manage turning them, but that didn't explain the knives. "What are the chances of Nathaniel recruiting a ghost to work for him?"

Tessa gazed at the ruined kitchen. "I'd say the chances are good."

Read more in Bleeding Hearts, Poison Garden #2

Also By Jennifer Allis Provost

Poison Garden

Belladonna

Oleander

Bleeding Hearts

Thornapple

The Chronicles of Parthalan

Heir to the Sun

The Virgin Queen

Rise of the Deva'shi

Golem

Elfsong

Sunfall

Pieces of Parthalan: Six All-New Stories From The Land Of Parthalan

Copper Girl

Copper Girl

Copper Ravens

Copper Veins

Copper Princess

Gallowglass

Gallowglass

Walker

Homecoming

The Winter's Queen Trilogy
Touch of Frost
Giant's Daughter
Elphame's Queen

About the Author

Jennifer Allis Provost writes books about faeries, orcs and elves. Zombies, too. She grew up in the wilds of Western Massachusetts and had read every book in the local library by age twelve. (It was a small library.) An early love of mythology and folklore led to her epic fantasy series, The Chronicles of Parthalan, and her day job as a cubicle monkey helped shape her urban fantasy, Copper Girl. When she's not writing about things that go bump in the night (and sometimes during the day) she's working on her MFA in Creative Nonfiction.

Follow Jenn on Patreon for exclusive content: https://www.patreon.com/jenniferallisprovost

For up to the date sale and new release information, follow Jenn on BookBub: https://www.bookbub.com/profile/jennifer-allis-provost